CW00433780

MELODY MAYHEM

RICHARD TEARLE

Cover design by
It's A Wrap

CONTENTS

FOREWORD

by Helen Hollick

Short stories are a thing of personal taste – love them or hate them. They are, however, excellent pass-times for short journeys, especially suited for the tedious daily commute or to accompany the morning coffee or afternoon tea break. I like to have a stock of short stories on my Kindle for idle time spent in waiting rooms prior to various necessary appointments.

There is a knack to writing short stories for they must all contain similar elements of format and expectation: they must interest the reader from the opening line, contain enough information to show what is going on, how, where, when and why, but not so much that the pace or feel of the story becomes swamped. A little mystery is good – that element of intrigue that keeps the reader glued to the page (or screen) to find out what happens next. And usually there is a neat twist at the end – the 'Well I didn't expect *that!*" syndrome.

A couple of years ago I coerced several friends (most of them authors, but not all) to contribute a short story or two to *Discovering Diamonds*, the historical novel review blog I run online. I wanted something as an additional entertainment for our blog visitors for the Christmas period and suggested we write something with a theme of 'diamonds'. The stories that came back were fabulous. I would never have guessed the diversity that can be included in a given theme!

The idea was a success, so for the following two years I again asked for short stories, only the theme was to be "A story inspired by a song or tune." These proved even more of a triumph, averaging over five-hundred visitors a day to the blog, all keen to read the next story.

Several of the best stories were contributed by Richard Tearle and Barbara Gaskell Denvil, and over lunch with Barbara and her daughter one weekday in a charming Exeter restaurant overlooking the Cathedral Green, we happened to mention Richard's talent for writing darn good stories. "He ought to put them into an e-book," one of us said.

So here we are, doing just that.

A couple of the stories added are by Barbara and myself, (our thanks to Richard for his generosity in including us,) but the rest are Richard's. Some, for us 'older folk' will stir memories – who remembers the evocative guitar playing of The Shadows and the like? Others will conjure youthful romance, 'oo-er' mystery, or even bring on a few tears. All are cleverly written, highly entertaining and just the right stuff for a good short story collection.

Enjoy!
Helen Hollick

INTRODUCTION

Many years ago, I was working in a taxi office. The days were long and ranged from busy to boring. I saw an advert for a local writing competition and utilised the time to start writing a book. The only criteria was that it had to be based predominately in the area. One of the drivers asked me what I was doing: without any further details I told him. 'Aw,' he declared, 'you'll never get that published.' Don't you love encouragement?

In the event, he was right. But it was selected for the long list of ten and then went through to the short list of five. I'd been writing short stories whilst attending Creative Writing courses during a fairly long period of unemployment. But then I got a 'proper job' (ironically, with the Unemployment Services!) and any ideas of writing were shelved. (Though I did write a 'Musical' based my exploits behind the desk at the Jobcentre and a never-to-be-performed Pantomime – Dick Waddington of Whittington!)

After eighteen years as a fairly Civil Servant, I retired and, inevitably, looked for something to do. That is, if I could fit it in between holidays, days out, babysitting duties with grandchildren etc etc. Purely by chance, I saw a post on Social Media asking if anybody was interested in reviewing historical fiction, written by Indie authors. Interested???

I applied, not expecting a reply, let alone an acceptance.

Enter Helen Hollick. She was my 'Boss' and I plagued the life out of her! A short while afterwards, she started her own review site – Discovering Diamonds – and invited me to join her. Suffice to say I jumped at the chance. After all, the Money was Nothing, but the Books were Free!

Since then, she has become my friend and my mentor. She calls me her 'senior reviewer' though that is probably based more on age rather than any particular skill!!

I shall now come to the point: every December on the site, Helen gives us reviewers the chance to show what 'we' can do by submitting a short story based on a song and I was delighted to have one published for each of the last three years. They were well received by my colleagues and quite a few others who read them. I was encouraged by all of this and began writing seriously once again.

A short while ago, Helen and another mutual writing friend had a 'meet-up' and for some reason, my name came up and my stories discussed. The daughter of the other writer was also present and, having a publishing company, offered to publish my stories! Believe me, the writing community is made up of some truly wonderful people. (But: never cross a writer else you may find yourself suffering a painful and humiliating death in their next book!)

This, then, is the result of those initial talks (over gin and/or wine, I suspect), so thank you Helen, Barbara and Gill.

PART ONE

Inspired by Classic Songs

OUR SONG

*This story first appeared on Discovering Diamonds
in December 2017
titled as 'Diamonds'*

JUST HEARING that Tony Meehan drum intro took me back to a cold February night in 1963. Back to that church hall in Friern Barnet, next to the Orange Tree pub. Back to the youth club where me, Mick, Jimmy and Paul were playing our first – and only, as it happens – gig supporting another local group, The Falcons.

And then, following Mick's faithful intro, I came in. It was our last number and I wanted to get it just right. Leave an impression. In order to try and capture the exact sound Jet Harris made with his revolutionary six-stringed Fender Jaguar Bass, I used a thicker plectrum – it gave the sound an authentic 'clunk' as I hit the lighter strings of my Guyatone standard lead and rhythm guitar. Cheap it was too, just four quid off a mate.

I had my stance and had been practising my facial expressions in front of a mirror. I closed my eyes and squeezed the notes out of the strings, fingers pressed heavily against the fretboard. I raised the neck of the guitar for the higher notes and dropped it for the lower ones. Front knee bent slightly; back leg straight, not unlike Gene Vincent. The notes dripped like melting chocolate. Paul – who never missed a chord change – kept the rhythm going; Jim plodded out a bass line. Mick's drums threatened to drown all of us out. Johnny Adams, our manager, fiddled with my amp to get more volume.

I ventured a glance at the crowd. Small but growing; they hadn't come to see us, after all. But they seemed to be enjoying our set of bog-standard instrumentals. The Shadows stuff, mostly. Obscure album tracks. We'd played *Walk, Don't Run* by the Ventures and that had been good, as had *Chariot* by Rhett Stoller. And an instrumental of *Where Have All The Flowers Gone* which Paul's dad had liked. A shame none of us could sing.

I stepped back from the mic, played softer and Johnny fiddled with the amps so that we almost recreated the fade out pretty well.

And it was over.

❟

I bought myself a Coke from the table selling soft drinks and crisps. I hadn't realised how hot and thirsty I'd become, and I demolished the drink in two long gulps.

"That was good," a voice said. Female.

I turned. She was blonde, about five foot five and had the most vibrant green eyes. Like emeralds. Diamonds. She wore a tight white sweater a flared short skirt and white knee length boots.

"Thank you," I said. "Er, would you like a drink?"

"Thank you. Coke. Please." Then: "I love that tune."

"Which one?"

"*Diamonds*. The last one. I like Jet Harris. My favourite Shadow. When he was with them," she added needlessly.

"Mine too." It wasn't just a line to attract more attention from her; it was true. The name, the really cool hairstyle. Jet was 'the man' in my eyes. I offered her a cigarette. Perfectos I smoked in those days. King size. Impressive, I hoped. She accepted and I held out my lighter for her. She bent her head, flicked her hair away from her face and then blew smoke out. "I'm Stephanie," she said. "Most people call me Stevie."

I told her my name. She smiled and said, "I know."

I took her arm and steered her away from the table, indicating a pair of lonely chairs on the other side of the hall. The Falcons were setting up.

"You're really good," she said, sipping her Coke.

I thanked her. I knew that I wasn't really that good, but I'd done alright tonight and was happy. No bum notes and only once did I finish a tune before the rest of the group.

The Falcons began their set. *Please, Please Me*. A song by a new group called The Beatles. Then an obligatory Chuck Berry number.

I sighed. "None of us can sing," I said. "We would do that stuff if we could."

"You don't have to be able to sing," she laughed. "I saw a group last week. The Rolling Stones. They can't sing!"

"But it's having the guts to stand on a stage and do it. That's the problem with us."

"Never mind," she said and looped her arm through mine. "It'll come."

"Do you live far from here?" I asked tentatively.

Stevie smiled and confirmed that she was only a few streets away.

"Can I – can I walk you home?"

"Later," she said. "Let's have a dance first."

We dropped our cigarettes onto the wooden floor and I ground them both out with my Cuban heeled Chelsea boots. As we progressed from a gyrating twist to a slow and smoochy number, I caught Paul's eye over Stevie's shoulder. He grinned and winked, and I gave him two fingers. But there was a smile on my face as I did so.

Later, in the chill of a dark February night, I walked Stevie home. Cloudy and moonless it was and the only stars to be seen were in my eyes. And hers, I noticed as we shared a first kiss outside her front door.

There were to be many more times that I walked her home; all carried the same magic as that first, wondrous night. After two years of courtship we became engaged and two years after that I made Stevie my wife. Our first solo dance at our wedding reception was to the tune of *Diamonds*. By special request.

We never really got anywhere with our music. Paul decided he would take on some vocals, so we changed our name from The Survivors to The Soul Survivors and again to The Purple Trolleybus (I kid you not!). It didn't work and we didn't actually get any gigs. Paul got into The Blues and we suffered from the inevitable 'musical differences' reason for splitting up.

Beside me all the time was Stevie. She came to all our rehearsals, offered words of advice and encouragement. When it went pear shaped, she told me to shrug my shoulders and walk away. She was right.

I still kept up playing – we had a lot of fun singing together and later to the kids when they came along. At some point, I joined a friend as a Country and Western duo. George had a terrific voice and, in all truth, we weren't bad and completed two summer sessions in a local pub. But that was as far as we got.

※

The oh so familiar tune came to its fading end, Jet Harris's bass still true after more than fifty years. I raised my head as an organ began to play and I stared at the coffin as it rolled away to the furnace. Stevie's coffin. The purple curtains closed silently, and I whispered a simple 'Goodbye, Stevie. Love you.' Tears blurred my vision and when I rose, I stumbled slightly. Hands supported me and I mumbled my thanks.

I was led outside. Another grey February day. Fitting, I suppose.

Someone somewhere whispered, "Strange choice of music."

But *Diamonds* had always been 'our song'.

♪

Song: Diamonds
Performers: Jet Harris And Tony Meehan
Writer: Jerry Lordan

WHAT PRICE FREEDOM?

This story first appeared on Discovering Diamonds,
In December 2018

I DREAMED of Bobby again last night. Roberta, that is. Roberta Mary McGee. Late of Macon, Georgia and now – well, who knows where.

We met in a bar in Baton Rouge where she was singing. Her voice was exquisite, but it was lost on the patrons. You would think that here of all places, where the Blues were born, she would have afforded some credibility. But all she got was polite applause and she was close to giving up. It was then I decided to help her. I remember climbing onto the stage, giving her a smile in return for her enquiring frown and slipped the harp out of my jeans. She understood and nodded. We exchanged a couple of words about songs and then I gave the standard five note blues riff. She picked it up on her guitar – I would soon find out that even that was borrowed for the occasion – and we launched into a Muddy

Water's song. At least the addition of my harp made the clientèle sit up and listen. Man, we rocked the place that night.

She wasn't stunningly attractive. Slender with very long legs poured into tight jeans; a faded black T-shirt with a bleached head-shot of Jim Morrison. Her hair was raven black – I swear it had a blue sheen to it – that hung straight to a point just below her shoulders whilst the untidy fringe flopped over her forehead, obscuring one, light brown, eye.

A few weeks later, the year ticked over from sixty-nine to seventy and the decade whispered away into faded memory. The bar closed down, owing us both money and we could find no work. Thanks to an obliging trucker we made it to New Orleans without getting too wet. But Bobby wasn't comfortable there and she wanted to go north again. I wanted to go west. We compromised: we went north.

But the coal mining towns of Kentucky were no more kind to us than those of the Deep South. Gigs were hard to come by, money even more so. And only then did Bobby relent and agree to go to California. "If we gotta sleep out in the open, might as well do it where its warm," she shrugged.

We hitched, we walked and, hell, we even rode a freight train until we were discovered and got thrown off. "You like the freedom?" I asked her as we slogged along the highway, sticking our thumbs out at every passing car. There wasn't many of them by the hour and none of them stopped.

"Freedom? Are you kidding me? What's freedom anyway? Ain't worth a bent cent. Only means you ain't got nothing to lose."

"I started out with nothing ..." I began

"And I still got most of it left," Bobby finished off for me.

"At least it's free," I murmured after a while. She punched me on the arm and pushed on ahead.

Later, lying in our only sleeping bag, Bobby turned away from me. "What do you want?" she asked. I sighed and rolled onto my back, resting my head on my elbow. This wasn't a simple question with an answer like 'a plate of rib steak with fries', or 'your body again'. This was a serious one. A deep question. One that required a lot of thought, mainly because I had never addressed it before. What did I want? I didn't know. Which is what I told her.

"You're useless," Bobby grunted. "What about love? Have you ever been in love?"

"Once," I said.

"Well, that's something". She turned to face me again. "What was her name?"

"Janey," I replied without thinking.

"How did you meet her?"

"College."

"Ah, college. Everybody falls in love at college."

"I guess."

"How did it end?" Nothing if not persistent.

"Usual way. Drifted apart. She went her way and I went mine. No big deal." We both knew I was lying.

"And you've never been in love since?"

"No," I blurted out hastily. Too hastily. "But I ..."

Bobby's cold fist thumped against my chest. "Don't say it." It was almost a snarl.

I shrugged. "You asked."

Bobby turned away again.

"What do I want?" I continued. "I'll tell you. I want the freedom that you seem to despise. I want to walk into a bar and play my songs and walk out with some money in my pockets. You wanna know why I want that? I'll tell you anyhow: it makes me feel good, Bobby. Hearing you sing, it's so easy to feel good. Best thing in the world. And I want to make records, maybe films, get my face on the cover of *Rolling Stone*, wear what I want, say what

I want." I took a deep breath. "I want a good wife, children. My own house and land. I want people to know my name and speak it as they say '*Howdy*' and shake my hand. And: I want you, Bobby."

Bobby didn't hear; she was asleep.

The next morning, I let her walk on ahead again. I was morose and in bad humour and if she said something I was liable to snap her head off. She sensed this, damn it, she *knew* it. You don't travel with someone for months without getting to know them. She knew my soul whether or not she knew all the details of my life.

But there was one thing she didn't know.

I wasn't good enough for her.

I knew it but she didn't. She'd argue, of course, but it was nevertheless true. She deserved better than me. A man who could give her the things *she* needed. The sort of life she wanted. I was not that man. I was a drifter, never able to settle, always moving on. Running away? Possibly. Always dreaming. Ever hoping. But never achieving.

"Goin' to Selinas, if you folks need a ride." The truck driver's voice broke into my reveries and I rushed to catch up and climb aboard.

Selinas. County seat of Monterey, California. Scene of Steinbeck's great novel, *East of Eden*. Hell, yeah, we'd made it!

And it was here, two months later, I let her go.

{

It's been fifty years since Bobby held my hands, kissed me on the cheek and apologised for falling in love with another man. I'm over seventy now and she? Well, not something I wanted to think about, but she may even be dead. I've been through it all, the booze, the drinks, the wives. The money. The cancer pains me and I don't know how many days I have left now, but there won't be many.

But you know what? I'd swap every one of them for just one night from the past.

One night of holding Bobby's body close to mine.

Song: Me And Bobby Mcgee
Performer: Kris Kristofferson
Writers: Kris Kristofferson And Fred Foster

CHIPS AND ICE CREAM

This story first appeared on Discovering Diamonds,
In December 2019

"JUDY!" my brother Keith called. "Don't be late."

I waved back, as if that were any assurance that I would not be. I was seventeen back then in 1965, my head full of teenage things; fashion, music and boys. Not that there had been many of those in the short years since maturity had painfully muscled its way in and thoughts began to turn to such things. I was the one with the pretty girlfriend and about whom one of any pair of hopeful lads would invariably say; "Don't fancy your one."

Not that I was ugly or anything. At least, I didn't think so. But I was short, had not yet lost all my puppy fat. My legs were not quite suited to a mini skirt; I tottered on stilettos. I was sparing with make-up; never too much but perhaps not quite enough. Boys did look at me, but only rarely twice.

I don't think I can put my finger on it, even now, but I felt a change in the air. I suppose it was mostly the difference between the morning when we had left London and now – early evening in

Margate. The family holiday. Regularly for the last ten years we had followed the A2 down to the Kent coast. No jetting off to exotic places in those days. The dubious delights of Ibiza or Malaga were almost unthinkable then. And I liked Margate. Some people may scoff at its blatant commercialism; the Golden Mile, souvenir shops, fish and chips. Dreamland. But there's more to Margate than that. A beautiful clock tower, the famous Shell Grotto, a sweeping sandy beach.

Dreamland was my destination now, running down the ramp that led to the cavernous entrance. The sweet smell of candy floss enfolded me immediately, like the embrace of a long-lost friend. I breathed it in along with the sounds of Rock 'n Roll that accompanied every ride, fading as the cars or the metal baskets that could hold three or four people slowed and shuddered to a halt.

This was the start of it all. Six days of heaven – seven if Dad had to go back to work on the Friday and he and Mum allowed Keith and me to stay on the extra night and take the train home the next day. Six days of sunbathing (though I was too conscious of my body to dare to wear a bikini) and six nights of riding the Dodgems, my favourite ride. I was learning to drive, so the practice would be good, I told myself.

And that is where I met him. Edward. Although I did not know that just then.

Like me, he could have done with losing a little weight, yet he leapt lightly onto the back of my car, held his hand out for the fare. It was my first ride, so I only had a ten-shilling note. "Be back in a minute with yer change," he said and jumped off without losing his balance. Cockney, like me, but a little more pronounced.

"You'd better be," I called out. I'd been shortchanged before. He looked back at me, smiled, winked placed the top of his forefinger against the end of his thumb, forming an 'O'.

Somebody rammed me from the side, a grinning idiot who didn't understand the word 'Dodgem'. I snarled at him and spun the wheel to get away. I heard the laughter as the car jerked away.

Del Shannon's *Runaway* melted in the night, drowned out by the klaxon and the hum of the electricity faded into silence. I remained in my car, watching as some left their cars, others refilled them and the money collectors pushed the empty cars to the side of the rink.

He did come back to me, proffered an assortment of silver coins – half crowns, shillings and sixpences. I checked them; he hadn't cheated me. "Stayin' on, darlin'?" he asked. I nodded, gave him the money. He shook his head. "Nah, 'ave this one on me. I'm off for a bit after this round - fancy some chips?'

He didn't wait for my reply, just winked again and told me to wait for him. I was nodding feebly, too shocked to actually voice my agreement. The klaxon sounded again, sparks flashed like fireflies around the overhead contacts and the Beatles claimed that it was *they* who wanted to hold my hand.

I drove like a novice. Cars clattered into me, jolting my bones. At one point I was stuck, pumping the accelerator pedal like a mad thing until I finally moved. But I didn't care.

That session seemed to last twice as long as normal, finished eventually. I climbed out, looked around. There he was, waiting, smiling, crooking his finger. I swear I was shaking.

He didn't put his arm around me, didn't even grab my hand; he just led me through the crowds to a van selling chips and all sorts, ordered two bags. I offered to pay my share; he pushed my hand away.

"Won't do my diet any good," I tried to make a joke of it.

"Why do you think you need to diet?" he asked through a mouthful of fried potatoes. I looked at him. He was serious. Not taking the mickey.

I shrugged, not wanting to get into any conversation about my figure. Instead: "Where are you from – er?"

"Edward. Eddie if you prefer. Which I do, to be honest. Edmonton. London. Not Canada." he smiled as if he had the need to explain.

"Judith," I replied. "Judy, if you prefer. Which I do." He laughed at my mimicry.

"And where does Judy come from?"

"Crouch End, North London. And there's only one."

"How long you here for, Judy?"

"Until the end of the week. Friday. But I may be able to stay and extra day. Depends on my parents."

"Mmm," he said, screwing the chip paper into a greasy ball, wiped his hands on his jeans and tossed it casually into a large waste bin a yard away. "Me too. Season ends on Friday night."

"What will you do?"

"Dunno. Might go to Brighton. A couple of weeks there before they shut down."

"Oh," I said. Was I disappointed that he wasn't returning directly to London?

We talked. Easily, uncomplicated stuff. He was neither forward nor shy. When he had to go and I had to fulfil my promise of not being late, he kissed me. Straightforward, neither passionate nor uncaring. No tongues. A perfect gentleman. Almost.

I didn't go to Broadstairs with the family the next day; I wanted time on my own. In the sun, with my book. With my thoughts. So when they left the guest house in Dad's green and cactus Triumph Herald, I made my way to the beach selected my hereditary spot near the sun deck, paid for a deck chair, set myself up for a morning (at least) of reading, reflection and relaxation.

But I couldn't concentrate on my book. The words blurred and I reread so many passages that made no sense that I put the book down in exasperation. It could wait, I had read it so many times that I almost knew it word for word.

I sank into the colourful canvas of the deck chair and closed my eyes. For early September, the weather was glorious; warm sun diffused by the gentlest of breezes. Edward. Eddie. What was special about him? Why did he make me feel this way? Indeed, what exactly did I feel about him? It couldn't be love; love grew, didn't hit you like an express train. The term 'crush' is well named; I felt as though my heart was squeezed from all angles. And it hurt. Even through closed eyes covered by sunglasses I saw his face. His expressions when he spoke, his lips when he smiled, his eyes when he kissed me. Ouch! My heart groaned as another barb lanced home.

I drifted into a snooze to a symphony of squawking seagulls, gentle surf, excited cries of children who surely should be back at school by now. Intermittent pop music from tinny transistor radios. For how long I lay like that I don't know, but I actually felt the shadow over my face. Even before he spoke, I knew who cast that shadow.

"Hi, 'ello Judy. Whatcha readin'?"

Be still my heart! Why did it jump like that? I wasn't a fan of Mills & Boon but suddenly I understood them so much better.

I removed my sunglasses and touched the open book resting cover upwards on my lap. "Jane Eyre," I said. "My favourite book. Ever."

Eddie sat down on the sand beside me. "Not my sort. I like some action. James Bond. Yeah. Sex, sadism and snobbery, that's what it says on the covers! Can I get you an ice cream?"

I perked up. "Let me pay," I pleaded. "You bought me chips last night, after all." I fished in my purse. Eddie stood up. "I'll go get them," he said as he took the money from me. What do you want?"

"A '99'," I confirmed.

"Right. Be back in a jiffy. Don't go away."

As if.

It was perhaps the loveliest afternoon of my life. We spoke and we sat in silence. The hours passed. We paddled in the retreating tide and he put his arm around my waist as I stumbled in the shrinking sand. We laughed and, briefly, we kissed again.

And then he had to go to work. We parted with a promise that we would meet up later. He'd take me around the fairground and have some rides; the Scenic Railway, the Waltzer, the Big Wheel. I watched his back as he walked away and that wasn't a tear in my eye, surely? Some sand had got in, probably. Yes, that would be it.

Every evening we spent in each other's company. Nights of fun, cuddles and kisses. But no frolics. We had more in common than I had thought. Was it enough? And now, Friday already. Mum and Dad had, as I had hoped, left for London and Keith and I stayed on for the extra night. The rooms were paid for anyway, I had argued, and they had acquiesced. Keith, a year younger than I, knew something was up with me and every day I had been treated to sniggers and winks. The parents failed to notice.

My heart was unbalanced. It was light and jumping in anticipation that I would see my love again. It was heavy because it was our last night. Nothing had happened between us. Unlike other girls I knew, we had not 'done it'. Not that there had been much chance; I could not take him back to the guest house and he did not invite me to ... to wherever he stayed.

I had already decided that I would stay until the fairground shut down for the night, shut down for the season. If I was being reckless, I didn't care about that either. I was determined to make the most of this night and if Keith breathed a word to anyone, I would kill him.

It was all I hoped it would be. I spent all my time on the Dodgems except when Eddie was on a break. His arm around my waist, he said "Kiss and Chips?" I laughed and obliged. But I could not hide the tears as the night wore on, skipping away from us.

I stood and watched as he finished his last shift, collected his wages and came back towards me. I was shivering, but not all of it was due to the night air. Something was slung over his shoulder. I cocked my head to one side. My heart failed to find a stable place to rest within me. A blanket.

"What's with ..." I began.

"Tradition of mine," he replied easily. "Last night of the season, sleep on the beach."

"And, er ...?"

"If you want to. I won't make you. Your decision. Do you want to?"

I did and, for the record, we did. There's not much of a harbour at Margate, but the stone pier afforded some lights and, from under the sun deck across the bay, we sat and watched the small fishing boats bobbing in the gentle waves, a narrow stream of moonlight shimmering on the sea, the silhouette of a tanker on the horizon. Playing in my head was the last song I had heard as we walked out of Dreamland: the Shirelles, *Will You Still Love Me Tomorrow'*. I knew how Carole King must have felt when she wrote it.

Love. It was love and I could not deny it. This was no mere crush; it was deeper than that. I had allowed him into my inner self; he knew my secrets as no one had ever before. He promised he'd write to me; it was the last thing he said to me in the morning. Could I believe him? Would he really? Or was this just another conquest for him? A holiday romance. Ships that pass in the night. A foolish girl and an experienced seducer? Two star crossed and frustrated lovers, my Columbine to his Pierrot?

There is an ending to my story; I quote my favourite book: *"Reader, I married him ..."*

Judy

Song: The Carnival Is Over
Performer: The Seekers
Writer: Tom Springfield

OF GHOSTIES AND GHOULIES AND
THINGS THAT GO BUMP IN THE NIGHT

THERE'S a Jimmy Dawkins in every town. You all know one; he's not bad, not even naughty, just, well, adventurous. Inquisitive. The type who would see a hole in a fence and climb through just to see what was on the other side. And if there was no hole, well, he might just make one if no one was looking. Jimmy was the boy who always ran everywhere, knocked on people's doors and promptly disappeared. Scrumped apples in the summertime.

Which is why the five of us, Jimmy, Willie Martin, Pete Holdsworth and me were squatting behind the wall that separated the old man's house from the green that bounded Hampstead Lane.

Jimmy was a natural leader; at thirteen he was a year or two older than the rest of us. We followed him; there was no question.

"He's a vampire," Jimmy assured us. "Remember that thunderstorm the other night? That was him. Flew out into the night and brought the thunder and the lightning in to cover him."

"Why?" asked Pete?

Jimmy snorted as if the question were a stupid one. "So he can find his victims," he explained patiently. "Man or woman, he sort of hypnotises them and he makes them vampires too."

"How does he do that?" Pete persisted.

"Haven't you seen any Dracula films?" Willie put in. "Christopher Lee?"

"Yeah. 'Course I have. But, but they're not real, are they?"

"Of course they're not real."

I wasn't the only one who almost jumped out of his skin. He stood there, leaning on the wall and looking over it, a smile on his face. A kindly, amused, smile that was not threatening in any way. "I've been waiting for you," he chuckled.

"F-for us?" I stammered.

He smiled at me "Well, not for you specifically. But inquisitive boys *like* you. It didn't have to be you especially." His voice was soft, with an accent that I couldn't place. But he sounded like the Germans do in war films when speaking English. "Come in with me boys. You can tell me what they say about me. And I will tell what is true! Perhaps I can offer you a sandwich and a glass of fruit juice. Hmm? What do you say?"

"I have to get back," Pete blurted out. "My auntie is coming round and I have to be there." We all knew that was a lie; Pete was even more of a wimp than I was.

"Then go you must," the old man said. "Perhaps you may pass on to these young men's parents that they may be a little late, but will be home soon."

Pete jumped to his feet and cried, "Yes, yes I will," before disappearing into the distance.

"Come, then, my boys, I'm quite sure you are all capable of climbing over the wall. It will save you walking around to the gate. Eh?"

I looked at Willie whose face was as pale as mine must have been. But Jimmy was already clambering over the rocky ragged edge of the wall. I shrugged and together me and Willie followed him. The old man was already yards ahead of us and now we saw the doorway he was heading for.

"Did you see his eyes?" Jimmy said. "Black as coal, I swear!"

"Never seen no one with black eyes before," Willie said.

"And he walks with a stick," I pointed to the hobbling figure ahead. "Wouldn't walk with a stick if he was a vampire, would he?"

"That's where he keeps his magic," Jimmy said, re-establishing his authority. You couldn't argue with Jimmy when he thought he was right.

"Come along boys! I declare you are slower than I am tonight!"

We hurried along arriving at the open doorway. Light flooded the narrow hallway. Electric light. What was I expecting? Candles?

"I have instructed my butler to fetch you some refreshment. I trust ham and cheese sandwiches will satisfy your youthful hunger? And washed down with lemon juice. Come, come, we'll sit in my study."

We followed to him to an oak panelled room with an old desk behind which he sat. He indicated the sofa – leather and soft, it sunk inward when the three of us sat down almost in unison. The old man seemed to be studying us, sizing us up. A smile on his face. What was he sizing us up for? His next meal?

The butler arrived, suitably dressed. A much younger man than our host, he wordlessly deposited four plates and glasses on a mahogany side table, bowed to us and then left as silently as he had arrived. With a gesture of his hand, the old man bade us eat.

"So, what is it that people say, boys? What calumnies have I been subject to?"

"Calumnies?" I asked, pushing a stray piece of ham back into my mouth."

The old man waved a hand. "A fancy name for lies. Slanders."

"They say you're a vampire," Jimmy blurted out. "They say you bring thunder out of the mountains, and lightning into the sky!"

"Like this?" said the old man and clicked his fingers. We jumped. Nothing happened. And he laughed. "Anything else?"

Jimmy had composed himself. The display, or perhaps the lack of one, made him bolder. "They say that dogs howl whenever you walk past. That you have a case made from the skin of a snake. That people see you and jump into the river. That we should always draw the curtains whenever you're out walking!"

He shook his head. "And you believe this nonsense?" He wasn't angry, but neither was he pleased to hear Jimmy's revelations."

"No, sir," Jimmy affirmed.

"You did, though." The old man shook his head. "So, let me tell you the truth."

For the next fifteen minutes or so, he gave us a brief story of his life. Born in Poland, fought in the resistance during World War II and later became a pilot for the RAF. Settled in England, collected antiques and became a dealer. Retired some twenty years ago. And no, he did not sleep in Highgate Cemetery where there had always been rumours of vampires, he did not drink blood and he was not the devil either.

"I trust you will correct any similar stories that you hear about me," he said after he had finished. "I would be most grateful. At my age it is most upsetting to hear these tall tales."

"How old are you, sir?" I asked, finding some courage.

"Do they not teach you mathematics at school? Let us assume that I was twenty years of age when the war broke out. In which year was I born?"

"Nineteen, nineteen," I gasped back. "That ... that makes you one hundred years old!"

"A little shy of that number, but yes, almost a century."

Then he sent us home.

{

Back in the house, the old man shook his head in bewilderment. The stories people made up! He rose from his seat and crossed the study to the window, opened it and looked out. The moon was full and grey, wispy clouds crossed its face. He listened. No dogs barked. A car slowed down as it approached the narrowing of the road at the Spaniard's Inn and then was gone. With another sigh and a silent chuckle, he called to his butler to tell him he was retiring for bed.

All was quiet.

Save for the shallow beating of leathery wings descending the stone steps to the cellar.

Song: The Old Man Is Down The Road
Performer: Credence Clearwater Revival
Writer: John Fogarty

PEG O' MY HEART?

THE DEAL CUTTER on Ramsgate Harbour was always a popular hostelry. Tonight was no exception: a ship was in and the crew more than intent on spending a large amount of their wages all in one night after more than two months at sea.

Peggy approached the table where four of the least raucous shipmates banged their mugs together and joined in the singing. She bent over to refill a mug.

"Now I remembers what were missin' from me pie, lads," a voice next to her roared out above the noise. "A nice pair o' dumplin's t' soak up me gravy!"

Of course she'd heard – and suffered - far worse yet still she blushed as pink as a rose. "Now then, Henry Jones, I'll have less o' that if'n you don't mind." The last word turned into a mild scream as he pulled her down onto his lap. With an exaggerated flick of his head, he indicated that his companions should bugger off, sharpish like. Exchanging winks and nods with each other, they did so.

Someone left the inn followed by a swirl of pipe smoke, replaced by a breath of fresh air. Then the door closed.

"Peggy, oh Peggy, my true love! You does me wrong, lass! Why, I would marry you t'morrer if'n you'd just say the word!"

"Marry you, Henry? Why would I do that? Look at you: you're all dirty, your clothes have seen far better days. And," Peggy sniffed the air, "there's a constant smell about you. Tar! That's what I smell. It's all in your clothes. It would take a hundred washes to get rid of that and I bet they haven't even had one. Besides, you'll be back at sea before I'd even got used to being called Mrs Peggy Jones. And whenever – or even if – you'd ever be bothered to come back, you'd be spending all your money in places like this. Oh no, Henry Jones, you'd be the last man I would marry. Now, let me be off and about me work." Peggy struggled to free herself from Henry's grip, but he held on fast.

"Ah, Peg, don't go just yet," he protested. "Listen a while. Yes, I'm ragged now an' dirty too, I'll grant ye that. But I came here straight from the ship just t'see you. I can buy new clothes, fine clothes t'make you proud o' me."

"Let go, will you? Ol' Sam'll be after me if I ain't servin' tables."

"I'm thinkin' o' givin' up the sea, Peg." He gripped her wrist tightly; she was still intent on getting away. "Growin' a bit too old, maybe. Tired when we're away for so long. Aches and pains." Still Peggy tried to break his grip. "But I ain't been foolish wi' me wages' all these years. Look here." With his free hand, Henry fished something from his pocket. "Look: silver. Bits and coins. An' that's not all: I got more things than just these." His voice dropped to a whisper. "I got gold, Peg. Lot's of it. All stored away safe, like. An' it's just for you an' me. I'm a rich man, now Peg. A very rich man indeed."

Suddenly Peggy stopped struggling, turned to face the sailor. He wasn't a young man, but neither was she exactly a blushing maid any more. His skin was the colour of walnut shells and his forehead just as wrinkled. His cheeks were ruddy and the short, white scar on his jaw added character to his face. *I could*, she thought, *do worse*.

"Oh Henry!" she exclaimed, no longer struggling. Placed her

rather large bottom back on his lap. "Have I never told you how much I love you? Oh, I do, I really do. My strong, handsome sailor boy!" She stroked his stubbly skin with the back of her hand. "Of course I will marry you! Has long been my desire to do so, didn't you know?"

Henry rubbed his jaw. "Is that so, now, m'dear? See now, I been a sailor nigh on all me life an' I sailed all the seven oceans, seen many an odd thing, I have. Learned many a lesson, too. An' one of those is to listen to what folk say the first time they say it 'cos that is most prob'ly what they really mean." Henry stood up, leaving poor Peggy struggling to keep her feet.

"I'm a simple man, Peggy. I likes to whistle and I own that I have a fair singing voice. I likes me fun and some may call me frolicsome, but, speakin' plainly, I don't give a single pin what anyone thinks o' me. So: stickin' to me principles, like, I just want to say that ye refused me first offer an' as I believe they were your honest thoughts, I will find another girl to wear my ring."

Shrugging off Peggy's frantic attempts to stop him, Henry Jones strode out of the inn, breathed in the fresh sea air and, turning first one way and then the other, decided that he might have better luck at the Northern Belle.

♫

Song: Saucy Sailor
Performer: Steeleye Span
Writers: Traditional, Arranged By Steeleye Span.

STICKS AND STONES

by Barbara Gaskell Denvil
This story was originally included in Discovering Diamonds
December 2019 Story song Theme – a story inspired by a song.

THE SHADOWS beneath the great stone bridge were deepening and the nineteen pillars stood pale and proud as night slipped over old London. The starling platforms which slowed the swirl of the river between the pillars and out towards the estuary were grazed by the bump of the wherry boats and barges. The bridge was too low for the great sea-going ships, but the tenders bringing in the cargo were busy every day and a few at night. Still the occasional splash of the oars could be heard by those living in the houses along the bridge or praying in the chapel. The squawking squall of the sea birds had faded as the gulls slept.

Yet on one of the central stones, starlings huddled tight into the depth of shadow, and chattering amongst, were three aged women, each partially hidden by a dark hooded cloak.

"Hubble, bubble, toil and trouble," said Winifred.

Mabel scowled. "I wish you'd stop saying that, Winnie," she complained. "It doesn't mean a damn thing, you know."

Winifred looked somewhat abashed. "Well, I have to say

something," she complained. "Otherwise I just sit in silence while you and Bossy Boring Bandy Belinda talk non-stop."

Belinda, shaking her curls within her hood, ignored these insults and addressed Mabel with haughty calm. "It's the coronation tomorrow," she said. "I was looking forward to the feast."

"What makes you think you'll be able to get a drink amongst the thousands there?"

"I can slip in without being noticed," Belinda insisted. "You can sit and go thirsty if that's what you want, but I intend inviting myself to the feast."

They all stared at each other. It took a little time to consider.

"No," said Winifred.

"Yes, definitely," said Belinda.

"I'm just not sure," said Mabel. "It's not an easy decision. Is the new king worth it?"

Surprising the others, it was Winifred who answered. "He's another Henry," she said. "He'll be the eighth. They seem to think he's strong and handsome. I heard he has red hair and he's as tall as the Keep at the Tower. Of course, everybody thinks he's wonderful just because he's taken over from his miserable father, who everybody hated."

"Oh, pooh," objected Mabel. "The last one was a miserable sod, but who knows if this one will follow his father and end up the same?"

"King Henry VII was an ugly old thief," said Belinda with feeling. "He sat in his counting house all day, counting out his money and trying to think of a way of getting some more. Well, after all the trouble he went through to try and steal the crown, it never did him much good. Oh yes, he got rich and bought some fancy clothes, and now he's made his son rich, but he never enjoyed himself except perhaps in bed with his wife. Now he's dead, and this son is good looking and jolly."

"Does that make him a good man?"

"And will it make him a good king?"

"Frankly, who cares?"

"Personally," Mabel decided, "I'm cold. Do we have to sit out here under the bridge? The wind is coming up from the east, and it's chilly. Can't we go into one of the back streets or find a court-yard, light a fire and keep warm?"

"People will complain if we light a fire," Belinda pointed out. "Fire is such a danger with all these silly little cottages with thatched rooves."

"Perhaps we could light a little fire here on the river," suggested Winifred. "No one can see us anyway."

Mabel stared at Belinda and Belinda stared back. "What? Three little old ladies huddle in secret under the bridge, warming their hands over a fire in the middle of the Thames River? No, people will see us and think we're witches or something."

"Well, we're not witches, said Winifred crossly. "

"Well, don't act like one," complained Mabel. "We can't help being old." She smiled a little sadly at her two friends, wrinkled necks beneath their cloaks, little wrinkled faces and wrinkled hands. She held out her own hands, seeing the sepia spotted signs of age, the wizened knuckles and the broken nails. "Poor little me," she smiled. "But age also brings wisdom."

"Maybe for you," nodded Belinda. "But not for Winnie."

Getting a little tired of this continuous stream of insults, Winifred struggled to her feet, but the starling base wobbled, and she sat down again in a hurry. "Humph," she said, half choking. "I think I'll go off on my own and find a more cheerful spot to spend the night."

"We could all try a monastery," suggested Mabel. "Sometimes they take poor people in for the night, and we're certainly poor. I mean, it's fairly clear we are poor old crones without a penny to our names."

"I liked the idea of lighting a fire," persisted Winifred. "I know I'm an ugly old thing, but everyone is at our age. Though I don't want to spend the night with nuns and monks, I'd feel very unwanted."

"We don't have to admit that we're not religious."

"Well, we could pretend. Otherwise, you seem to think we look like witches. I object to that. I certainly don't act like a sick old witch."

Belinda laughed. "Now then, let's work out something sensible, since we want to be ready to watch the coronation and join the feast."

}

After a long chilly hour of argument, Winifred, Belinda and Mabel trailed from the river to the stabling sheds behind the tavern on the corner of Thames Street, and snuggled in beside the horses. This was certainly warm. The horses weren't very pleased at first, but they put up with it and even when the old ladies pinched most of the straw, they accepted their fate, and everyone fell asleep snoring.

The following morning they could already hear the cheering, the slap and crack of the bright painted banners hanging from every upper window, splashing their colours in the breezes. The king would ride from his royal apartments within the Tower, and slowly cross the mile from one side of London to the other.

The noise and pageantry were glorious, and the guards in their scarlet livery, followed by all the lords and ladies of the court who waved and smiled at everyone. The crowds lined every street as the king trotted through the widest of the cobbled roads, nodding and raising his hand as the citizens of London in their thousands came to cheer and clap and dance in the roads after the great procession had passed by. Minstrels played and even the king could be seen tapping his feet within the stirrups.

Standing well back behind the excited crowds, Mabel, Belinda and Winifred peeped between the heads of those crowded in front of them, watching as his royal majesty, King Henry VIII made his glorious way to Westminster Abbey on the other side of the city. All the gates stood wide open, folk hurried out from the taverns and inns, raising their cups of ale to the bright young king, and toasting his good health and long reign.

"Yes indeed," mumbled Winifred from the back of the crowd along Cheapside. "He's young, red-haired and handsome, and quite slim too, though I'd wager that won't last once he has all those feasts and cups of best wine."

"It's a shame we can't get close enough to him for a nice warm kiss," nodded Mabel.

Belinda cackled and waved her own hand to the king. He sat high on his beautiful black gleaming horse, keeping his speed slow in order that all his new subjects would have a chance to see how inspiring, grand and attractive he was. And they certainly appeared to agree. The previous king had certainly received no such accolade.

Everybody from young to old, from lord to beggar and from wealthy to baby, was dressed in their best. Winifred, Belinda and Mabel had no best clothes, and could only wear their big dark cloaks as they always did, a little stained unfortunately after all the years. But warm enough and hooded to keep their sad old faces in shadow.

"I wonder what our new king will look like in his crown," murmured Belinda.

"You'll never know," Winifred answered. "We certainly aren't invited into Westminster Abbey for the coronation. And after that, he'll travel straight to the palace."

"Ah well," sighed Mabel. "We can dream. These special occasions are such fun.

"As long as we can join the feast," added Winifred.

"Well," Belinda pointed out, "No one is watching us, and no one will because they're all too busy watching the procession and listening to the music. So we can creep in and feed all we want to."

"Right," Winifred said, pushing forward a little. "I want that woman over there in the pretty grey velvet dress. The one with the lace collar, and her neck well displayed. Then I'm going to move on to the man with the big nose over there – look. He looks perfect, he won't even hear me sneak up behind him."

"I think," said Mabel, looking around carefully, "I like the very young man standing on the other side. He's so excited he's jumping up and down. He certainly won't see me. Or perhaps I'll trip him and then take my feed as I help him up, and he'll just think I'm being kind. And his blood will be all simmering and fizzy from excitement. Then I'll find someone else if I'm still hungry."

Belinda grinned, mouth closed, hiding her vampire's teeth. "I want that fat woman with the basket of fruit. She's fat enough to fill me in no time, and her gown is cut so low I can suck her neck without even a shadow in the way."

"Now," Winifred nodded. "Now is the perfect time. And we can meet up afterwards under the bridge.

⟡

Song: *Under The Bridge*
Performers: *Red Hot Chili Peppers*
Writers: *Anthony Kiedis, Flea, John Frusciante & Chad Smith*

THE SONG'S GOTTA COME FROM THE HEART

RUPERT STOLE a glance at the large clock high above his head. Ten more minutes and he could take a break. A cup of coffee for his dry throat, a cigarette for his nerves, a shot of insulin for his diabetes. His fingers danced across the keys of the white grand piano, the notes quiet and not intruding into the thoughts, conversations or preoccupied minds of the early Christmas shoppers. Few took any notice of him. Like a machine he segued from *The Alley Cat Song* to *Love is Blue*. Muzak from human hands. Tunes that were catchy but ultimately annoying to both himself and the customers who barely listened anyway yet would find themselves humming or whistling something that they neither recognised nor realised they were doing so. Subliminal sales pitches. He closed on *Up, Up and Away*, suitably cheerful yet not thought provoking. A flourish on the final chord and then he closed the lid and stood up.

Outside, Rupert stood in the alleyway, insulin administered, takeaway coffee in his hand and a cigarette between his lips. The smoke coiled into the cold air.

"Rupert! I thought I'd find you here."

The store manager, John Mason. A tall man with a military bearing. Old fashioned pencil moustache. Impeccably dressed: a flower in the buttonhole of his dark suit.

Rupert nodded. He didn't really fancy a conversation with anyone at this time, but Mason was his boss. And Rupert felt that if there was to be conversation to be had then it might be one he would rather not have heard.

He was right.

"I've just had a long chat with Head Office," Mason began. "Bad news, I'm afraid. For you, that is. I mean, I'm sorry, I tried very hard to dissuade them, but they were insistent. I -er- I'm afraid that I have to terminate your employment here. Very sad. I did try. So close to Christmas as well. You're a pleasant young man and I shall be sorry to see you go. Truly. And so talented. I used to tickle the ivories a bit myself when I was younger. Not like you, though."

Rupert flicked the cigarette end away and automatically reached for another. "When?"

"When? When do you finish, you mean? Well, to be honest, once you have finished for the day, I'm afraid. Er – if you would call by my office, I will have a handsome pay out for you. Agreed by Head Office and I think you will find that all is in order. Plus a little bonus from the store, a way of saying thank you."

Rupert bit back the retort *Am I supposed to be grateful?* simply nodded and drew on the freshly lit cigarette. "I'll be there," he grunted.

"Yes, well, er ..." Mason stammered. "Well, I'll see you later then. Don't be late back!"

If it was meant as a joke, Rupert did not find it funny.

In all honesty, it came as no surprise to Rupert. It was nothing that he had done. Just company policy. It had been a prodigious gig: Bourne and Hollingsworth was one of the more well-known old style department stores in Oxford Street and when the opportunity presented itself to perform for the customers on a daily basis, he'd jumped at it.

It hadn't been quite how he had expected it to be. The white suit, ruffled shirt and black bow tie wasn't his normal attire by any means, but it was part of the contract. The piano, too, was white and therefore too showy for Rupert's taste. Alright, the money was good – or so it seemed to a student such as Rupert. Coming, too, just as the summer holidays arrived was most fortuitous. He was in his last year at the RSM – the Royal School of Music – wondering if he should stay at the job or complete his studies. Well, it was academic now.

What had surprised and annoyed him was the material. Whilst he had, to an extent, virtual *carte blanche* on his content, there were very clear guidelines; nothing too 'heavy', nothing too 'poppy', nothing too 'contemporary'. Nothing too 'jazzy'.

"They want to hear you, lad," Mason had instructed him, "but they don't want to *listen* to you." Rupert was also informed that he could play for an hour and a half, take a break and then restart his repertoire from the beginning. Then lunch, play, afternoon break, play. Rupert soon discovered that whatever charms *Take These Chains From My Heart* might ever have had soon paled.

He ground out the cigarette beneath his highly polished shoes. Slowly, and five minutes late, he pulled on the entrance door and returned to the store. He stopped to go to the lavatory, washed his hands, took his place back at the piano. Looked around him. Mason had been right. Customers hurried from one department or another, or made their way to or from the lifts, the toilets, the cash desks. The exits and entrances. They barely noticed him and certainly no one was waiting for him to start playing. Nor would they know that this was to be his final performance.

His fingers hovered over the keys, as reluctant as his mood to strike the first chords of bloody *High Hopes* yet again. Even if it was for the last time. The last time ever, Rupert decided. He would never play that song again if he lived to be a hundred!

Instead, he lightly feathered two notes, repeated them. *Fur Elise*, soft and soothing, slid effortlessly from his nimble and flexible fingers. Elgar's *Nimrod* rose into the air, seeking his prey, *Clair de Lune* tinkled out almost tearfully.

Rupert upped the tempo with the *Warsaw Concerto*, brightened it with *Ode to Joy* and completed the segment with *Bach's Fugue in D Minor*, always a stirring piece for him.

He breathed easier. If he had broken the rules then so be it: sheep and lambs came to mind as he played some of his mother's favourites, standards, she called them. Porter, Novello, Gershwin. Cahn and Van Heusen. His private joke: *Call Me Irresponsible.*

And then some jazz: the tricky but catchy *Take Five* – yes even if it was written in five flats! Nina Simone's *Feelin' Good* and *Black Coffee*, a couple of Julie London numbers, *Cry Me A River, A Nightingale Can Sing The Blues* and then Peggy Lee's *Fever.*

Time passed though he did not notice it. His head never rose once, his eyes stared resolutely at the keyboard, mesmerised by his own fingers dancing across the keyboard. Instinct alone told me that his final performance was close to being over. A quick glance at his watch confirmed it. Well, that was nice while it lasted! Time to end it, he thought: why not go with a bang?

Pausing only for a second, his favourite piece, Gershwin's *Rhapsody In Blue,* thundered out, rose in pomp, declined with grace.

It was over. The notes lingered for a moment, faded and died. Eyes closed, Rupert threw his head back and exhaled heavily.

His ears, still full of music, detected a growing sound, one that he had never heard in this place before.

Applause.

༉

SMELL THE WHISKY

"JOHN LEE? John Lee? What you doin' out there, honey, sittin' on the porch all alone in the dark?"

"Nothing', darlin'. Just sittin' here with a beer and thinkin'."

The night was hot and sticky, the setting sun casting long shadows on the bone-dry dirt track that led out to the highway. Bobby Jean flicked her dark hair away from her face.

"What's up, darlin'?" Bobby Jean asked. She sat beside him on the swing and snaked her arm around his shoulders. "Come on, baby, what's on your mind?"

John Lee ran his hands through his thick hair and lit a cigarette for her. She took it and inhaled deeply. "Ten years," he said quietly. "Ten years."

"Ten years? Since what, John Lee?"

He ignored the question. Took a pull from his beer. "My Granddaddy started it all. Runnin' the moonshine. He was a John Lee, too, y'know. Both him an' my Daddy. Now me. I'm the third John Lee Pettimore in succession. I weren't very old when the government tried to stop Granddaddy and his like. The Revenue Men they was called then. Tried to shut Granddaddy down, went chasin' down the holler determined to catch him at it and have enough to put Granddaddy away in the Pen. But the first one never came back. The Revenue Man, I mean. Must've had an accident or somethin', 'cos they never sent another one." He looked sideways at Bobby Jean. The newest woman in his life.

Bobby Jean sucked on her cigarette, blue smoke coiling in the still air. She didn't speak.

"My daddy ran the 'shine for him. I remember the car – a Dodge, big and black it was. Daddy found it at auction. Real run-down it was then, but Daddy had a way with engines." John Lee chuckled. "Had the damn cheek to paint 'Johnson County Sheriff' on the sides, blacked out the windows with primer. Couldn't see a damn thing inside."

Somewhere, a dog barked.

John Lee threw his cigarette onto the ground, killed it with his boot heel and promptly lit another. He leaned back on the swing seat and stared up at the darkening sky. He looked at Bobby Jean. She was a good girl. Accepted him for what he was. And she had a great body, too. He smiled at her. "Daddy and my uncle Billy Wayne set that Dodge up real nice like. Just over there." John Lee pointed to the old shed beside the house. "Tore that engine apart and tooled it up real good. Ain't nothin' ever gonna catch *that* son of a bitch. Man, that *sound* was somethin' else! Grumbled like a dog straining at the leash. Still gives me the shivers." He lapsed into silence again.

"Wanna 'nother beer?" Bobby Jean asked. John Lee nodded. He watched as she hauled herself out of the seat, mesmerised as her hips swayed from side to side in those tight blue jeans, shook his head at the fluidity and poetry of her movement.

He looked up when she returned.

"I must've been sixteen when the sheriff came round and told Momma they'd both died in a crash. 'Course, Sheriff Goodwillie knew all 'bout Granddaddy's li'l operation. A couple o' cases of good moonshine does wonders t'help eyes to turn the other way." John Lee took the cold beer from her, raised the bottle as if in salute and downed half of it in one long slug. He belched and smacked his lips. "Takin' the weekly load down to Knoxville, they were. Daddy and Billy Wayne. I weren't there, 'course, but they said you could smell the whisky burnin' for miles around. Granddaddy took it on himself real bad. Couldn't do enough for Mama, but she never blamed him for it."

They sat in silence. Drinking and smoking.

"Is that when you went to 'Nam?"

John Lee shook his head. "Not right then. Too young. Signed up two years later. My eighteenth birthday." He took another slug and laughed. "White trash, we were. Didn't matter if we got killed. So they flew us out right away. Hardly any training, just got us out there as soon as they could. But I finished two tours out in 'Nam. Someone up there musta liked me, 'cos not many of us got back home, y'know."

Bobby Jean pulled his head down to her shoulder and kissed him on the cheek. "I'm sure glad you made it, John Lee."

"Yeah, me too, darlin'," he replied and stroked her hair.

"Is that where you got the idea?" Bobby Jean asked.

"Guess so. It was crazy out there. Real crazy. When we weren't out in the field, we just sat around the camp, listening to The Doors, Credence, all the best bands, y'know? Someone always had some grass so we smoked that too. So, yeah, it was then I was thinking about a new operation. Met some guys. Bad guys. Made the contacts."

John Lee shifted in his seat and lit up again.

"Columbia," he continued, "they said. An' Mexico. Them's the places to get the seed. All y'all need was a place to grow it. Cultivate it. The ol' holler was perfect. No more havin' to distil the whisky. Just grow the seeds an' ship it out. Bigger market, bigger stakes. Bigger money."

"Ain't you afraid, John Lee?"

John Lee laughed. "What, 'cos the DEA got a chopper now? Nah, darlin', spent a lot o' my time in 'Nam ridin' choppers, looking out for Charlie. Still gives me the nightmares, but, hell, I learned a lot out there. That man comes snoopin' round here, he'll find out exactly what I learned."

John Lee looked up. The sky was black now with only a few stars beginning to show through, tiny light bulbs sewn into a velvet curtain. There was no sound to be heard except for the rasping of their breath.

"An' if he does find out, well, he won't be goin' back to tell anyone, now will he?"

}

Song: *Copperhead Road*
Performer: *Steve Earle*
Writer: *Steve Earle*

PIZZA PALACE

By Helen Hollick
Based on a True story...

WILLIAM PRICE SAT in the dark, elbows on knees, head cradled in his hands. He could hear the distant rumble of traffic and the footsteps of people hurrying past; overheard the occasional word as couples or groups of friends walked past. Most were snippets that had no relevance, but the occasional short sentence hit home, stung.

He sighed, stood, wandered around the empty restaurant, touching here and there a table, a chair. Where had it all gone wrong? When?

Several Months Earlier...

The press, journalists, local TV, people laughing, talking, drinking – they were over-spilling into the river-side street now. Success was not the word, this was phenomenal! In a daze William went around, squeezing between groups of people, nodding, laughing,

42

sharing a few words, a joke, as he topped up champagne glasses. Where was Zandra with those canapés? Ah, there, emerging from the kitchen with a fresh batch. He had never, ever, known of an opening night like this!

Mind you, were he to be cynical, it was more likely the free booze and bites that had attracted everyone. Still, all marketing counted: free for them, expensive for him but it would all be tallied against profit so might keep his tax bill down when it came to the required self-assessment. For now he was going to dwell on the fact that his newly opened Pizza Palace had the making of doing well. Prime location, staff who didn't expect a high wage and a chef who knew how to make pizzas. Sort of.

OK, so Zandra was an illegal immigrant with limited English. So what? The chef was his lazy brother whose only talent was for eating pizzas rather than making them – but the location was definitely prime. A few doors down was the best nightclub in town and this was right on the river front. With, as an added bonus, no fish and chip, Chinese or Indian takeaway shops near by. Hungry punters would flock to the Pizza Palace, and judging by the crowd here tonight, the publicity would be of benefit for quite a few months to come. There were one or two sarcastic comments from a couple of the female journalists, but he pretended not to hear. Snooty cows, they ought to stay at home and cook hubby's dinner not sponge for free booze.

A comment appeared on Facenote that night from an anonymous profile named 'I Am'.

"Call yourself a journalist, you old bat? You couldn't even write a shopping list on a roll of bog paper."

Three Months Later

"Look, Matt, we need some different toppings. People are getting fed up with the same-old menu."

"You want 'em, you make 'em."

William sighed, his brother had started slipping into these surly couldn't-care-less moods a few weeks ago. The months before had been fine, all seemed well out in the kitchen, turnover seemed steady, the customers happy enough. OK, there were one or two slip-ups – they were stupid Zandra's fault, serving a meat-feast pizza to that irritating Veggie girl who thankfully never came in again after that incident. Lord, you'd think she had been poisoned the way she had shrieked and started hurling abuse about the place. Silly cow shouldn't have posted a bad review on TripTalk though should she? She'd been easy to trace from there to Facenote. He'd laughed outright at the comment left for her by 'I Am' – an image of a girl stuffing her face with a greasy leg of lamb, accompanied by *'Maybe you need to eat meat dearie – no way are you gettin' any sex, you miserable cow.'*

He chuckled at the memory, then sighed again, looked at his brother. "All I ask, Matt, is for us to serve a couple of things a little different. To keep interest going."

Matt sniffed, wiped his nose on the back of his hand then continued making the dough for the evening pizzas.

"I'll add a different cheese."

William smiled, patted his brother's shoulder. "That'll do fine. Thank you."

Two Months Later

"You stupid girl – can't you even get an order straight?" Another wrong order delivered to the wrong table. Not Zandra this time, she'd long gone, had walked out in the middle of her shift for no apparent reason. So William had been undercutting her pay, so what? She was lucky to have got the money he had paid her. He'd enjoyed seeing that Photoshopped pic of her in the almost-nude on her Facenote page though a few days after she'd gone. *'This is what slutty illegals look like in the nuddy!'* It had turned out that she wasn't an illegal, or an immigrant. He couldn't care less. She wasn't a very good waitress either.

This new Lithuanian girl spoke little English, enough to – in theory – take orders from customers. Of course, to be totally fair it could have been Matt who had mixed the order up. He'd have a word later, after closing. No point now or the lazy sot would down tools and then they'd be up the creek without a paddle... Hey that gave him an idea! What if they ditched these cheap china plates that were so easily broken? Two women had complained last week about noticeable cracks. As if a crack mattered! He'd chuckled at the comments that then appeared on their Facenote pages – why did these people leave themselves so open to being found so easily on social media? They were just asking for the sort of comments they deserved. Serve these two right for putting their negative feedback on TripTalk – how dare they say bad things about him and his Pizza Palace? Bloody snotty women.

"Matt," he announced, pushing his way through the swing door into the kitchen. "We're getting rid of the china and buying wooden paddle boards as plates instead. I can get them at a good price on GBay."

"Paddle boards?"

"Yeah, pizza boards. So I can belt you round the head when you drink too much."

One Month Later

So the quality of the pizzas were not as good as they had been originally, but the punters would never know that William now bought them frozen in a job-lot from that cheap Italian supermarket twenty miles away. Once the packaging had been destroyed – well, dumped on the other side of a hedge in a field en-route home – who was to know they weren't fresh home-made pizzas? Maybe there weren't as many tables filled of an evening as there once had been, but that was that silly Polish tart's fault. Lord but she was so slow as a waitress!

She'd have to go – along with a few choice words about her flat chest and buck teeth on her Facenote page. Maybe he should get a different chef? Nah, Matt had his faults but his wages were mostly in booze and the other occasional packet of stuff. He was cheap to keep.

William forced a smile as that drippy pair of students finished their meal and left – left half their garlic bread as well. Didn't matter, he could split it up and serve it as individual slices to the next person.

He groaned. The next person was that batty woman from the other side of the river. He'd seen her dozens of times lately, walking past or sitting on that wooden bench on the opposite side of the river path staring at the Pizza Palace – at him. She had never come in before. Why start now?

"Good evening madam," after all these months he had the false smile and gracious tone off-pat. "Would you care to sign our visitor's book?" He took it off its stand, handed it to her along with a pen. "Just your name and email. We have a monthly prize draw. Winner gets a free meal."

The woman added her name, but nothing else. "Who won last month?" she asked as she handed the book and pen back.

"A Mr Tromp from the next town," William answered, putting the book away so that she couldn't be tempted to check. It was a lie, of course, no one ever won but it came in handy to use the little ruse to get people's names. It was then so easy to find them on Facenote.

She seated herself at a table in the corner, studied the menu. "Are these pizzas made on the premises?" she asked sweetly.

Too sweetly.

William retained his smile. "Oh yes madam, Chef makes the dough fresh." A sudden thought. She wasn't an Inspector, was she?

"I can recommend the four cheese Margarita with fresh salad as a side."

"Very well, I'll have that then. Thank you."

William almost felt like asking for her money in advance. It wasn't as if she looked homeless or anything, but she wasn't exactly new-looking either. Sort of dishevelled and shabby. With an old felt hat that flopped down over her face.

Had she read his mind, caught his disapproving expression? She indicated her worn, faded dress and old shoes. "I've been busy digging all day," she said.

William, nodded and indicated that the waitress should take over serving. He saw that the woman had taken a notebook out of her patchwork bag and was scribbling something. What excuse could he make if she was an inspector and wanted to see the kitchen? It wasn't *quite* as spotless as it should have been... Nothing for it, he'd have to get rid of her as soon as he could.

"Oh," the woman said, surprised, "You use wooden platters? How quaint. We used to have these back in the middle-ages. I'm surprised you don't have stale bread trenchers as well."

William drew himself up to his full annoyed height and sniffed loudly. "These, madam, are modern pizza accessories. Every trendy restaurant has them. They are state of the art."

The woman laughed – it sounded more like a cackle to William's ears. "They're certainly state of something, young man, but not art!"

She ate most of the pizza, leaving the crusts. No tip, William noted as she left. He watched her walk along the river path and cross the bridge. "Batty old witch," he muttered. Noticed that a wind had got up outside, rubbish was being swirled along the river path, had caught in a pile in the doorway, the door itself giving a little rattle.

Two days later he put a post up on Facenote. It was a good one.

"Batty old witch, keep your spells to your dirty old notebook. With any luck you and it will get burnt and roast in that place

downstairs." Added in his usual smattering of inelegant expletives and foul 'f' words.

The next day, on opening his laptop and checking his Facenote page he found a responding comment from 'Anonymiss', accompanied by the profile image of a woman's face hidden beneath the shadow of a witch's Halloween hat:

"Eye of toad, wing of bat, magic spell and black, black cat. Everything that is not nice - did you know you've got some mice?"

Beneath it another comment: *"Everything returns Threefold. Remember that."*

"Bloody woman. I know who this has come from!" He stabbed the delete button a few times, but could not remove either message. He hit 'block' but the laptop crashed. He'd have to reboot. The telephone rang, distracted, he forgot all about it.

One Week Later

They found a mouse's nest and dozens of droppings beneath the kitchen sink. The silly Polish girl had screamed and shrilled that she'd seen an actual mouse scuttle across the floor. Idiot. She'd not turned up for work this evening and the place was full again. Still, that cat hanging around in the back alley might be useful. Bit of a pity it was an unlucky black, but as long as it caught the mice...

Run off his feet, William did not get a chance to log in to Facenote until they had closed up for the night. It was well gone midnight. He and Matt shared the untidy, small flat upstairs, so thankfully no walk or drive home – especially thankful as Matt had been hitting the booze again. William had passed off his drunken singing earlier in the evening as, "My happy Chef, singing a few Italian arias as our little business is doing so well."

Before he went to sleep he decided to put something scathing on the Facenote page of that pompous old biddy who'd muttered loudly, "Sounds more like a cat with its tail shut in a door to me."

He opened his laptop. There, on his page, another comment from Anonymiss.

"Mice can do the scaring, but rats are far more daring. The trap is set – but which rat will we net?" "Onefold. Twofold. Threefold."

The next morning the kitchen had four dead rats in it. Two on the floor, one on the work surface, one in the food cupboard. How had they got there? The doors and windows were locked. No one could have got in.

Hastily William cleared up and cleaned round. Matt was still snoring; no new waitress had yet been found. No one would know. He tossed the dead rats out into the alley – further down by the fire exit of the night club. The cat was sitting there in the morning sunshine, washing its paws.

"You could damn well do your job instead of preening," William muttered.

He found time during the mid-morning coffee break to leave a quick, sarcastic comment for Anonymiss. *"What you're doing is trolling you miserable old bat. It's illegal. It's harassment, and I'll have the cops on you!"*

He tried blocking her again. To his surprise, that night when he logged on again, the block had mysteriously been unblocked.

A message read, *"Don't you like this game after all? What a pity, I was just starting to enjoy myself."*

Somehow word about the rats leaked out to the Inspectors. They searched the premises, dining area and kitchen. No mice. No rats, but William had never seen the cockroaches before. Nor had any idea that stupid Matt had been using condemned horse-meat for the meat-feast platters. Nor that those damn wooden paddles they served the food on were made from a foreign wood that carried a poisonous resin.

He stood in the dark. The CLOSED sign showing on the door. It would not be turning to OPEN ever again. He and Matt would be lucky to get away with a huge fine, but would probably get a jail sentence. Multiple charges, including possession of Class A drugs.

He wandered to the restaurant's window and peered out. People hurrying by did not look in at him but their words had already hit home.

"Surprised no one was poisoned."

"Oh, he used a different poison, that one – poison pen words from what I hear."

The worst thing, the very worst thing. They had confiscated his laptop. Not that it mattered, Facenote had banned him for sustained, vindictive trolling. Him! Bloody cheek! What about that 'Anonymiss' eh? What about *her* nasty comments?

William began to pull the blind down, to shut the world out. Noticed as he did so the black cat sitting outside. It flicked its tail, got up and walked along the river path, then over the bridge. Walked up to a woman dressed in shabby clothes and a felt hat that looked every inch like a floppy witch's hat.

She pointed to her own eyes with two fingers, then to him with three extended fingers outspread.

"What you give returns threefold Master Troll. Do not play a game if you do not like the rules."

Song: Games Without Frontiers
Artist: Peter Gabriel
Writer: Peter Gabriel

PART TWO

Other Stories

WINDOWS

THE PLACE where I live has just four windows. They are alike in size and shape, but they are very different in other ways.

Let us number them. Window One is fitted with plain glass. I look out over an ordinary street with grass verges and telegraph poles. A bus stop with a shelter is across the street. A tree obscures the dwelling directly opposite. Cars and other vehicles go and having gone, return and rest. Should you be passing and I happen to be sitting at my seat and looking out, there are things you will learn about me. That I have brown hair and eyes of a similar shade. That I am a male. That I am clean shaven, at least at that time. Nor do I wear spectacles when I sit at my window. You will not know if I need to wear them for reading. You will know, too, that I am Caucasian. You may be able to guess my age – give or take a few years either side.

This is all you will know about me as you pass by my window. You will not see whether I am tall or short, overweight or stick thin. The room is empty aside from my chair. You will not see bookshelves behind me nor a television set. You will not know my tastes. The only way you will ever know anything about me is if I invite you into my home and your own eyes will answer some of those questions without the need for speech. If I speak to you, you may guess my origins by my accent, but you will not know what part of that town, city or even county where I grew up.

Unless I tell you these things, all you will ever know about me is what you observe and what I tell you. Anything else is hearsay or lies.

Window Two. The outside pane is frosted; I can see out, but you cannot see in. You may be standing right by it and I will know if that is so. But you will not know whether I am even there. I can observe you and know more of you that you know of I. In all truth, it is not a particularly interesting window. It can, however, preserve my privacy whilst I invade yours.

I move on. Window Three is the opposite of Window Two. I cannot see out but you, you sir or madam, are permitted to see me. Not that there would be much to observe other than myself. But it is possible that you may see things that I cannot. Do I have a nervous tic in one eye or the other? Do I have a habit of rapidly tapping my heel upon the floor when thinking? Things that are so commonplace to me that I am no longer even aware of them. I no longer notice them: but you may. I do not often sit at this window.

Allow me, just for the moment, to return to Window One. I am a private person, but not a recluse. If it is a summer's day and the window is open, we may converse. I may even offer my name or other details. Only then will you gain more knowledge of me. Perhaps I will invite you in after all and offer more insights into who I am. Who knows: I may take you through to Room Two where more conclusions may be made. But always be careful: a room full of books and bookshelves does not actually mean that I can read. It is a fair assumption, but not always a given.

To admit you into my world is my choice. Thus far, all I have told you of myself is that I am male with brown hair and eyes and prefer privacy. That is all. Do not assume things about me that may not be true. Not until you can confirm them beyond doubt. Do not assume that you know what I am thinking or what I am interested in. That – and so many other things – is for me to tell you and not for you to guess however accurately, however wildly.

And so to Window Four. The most difficult and complex of them all. For I can not see through it and nor can you. Within the room behind it are my darkest, innermost secrets. I never sit at this window for it has a latch and what I may unleash by releasing the catch frightens me. Things so deep inside me and long since suppressed that I no longer acknowledge them. I no longer know they are even there. But some things are there nevertheless. Perhaps one day they may be unleashed. A trigger word or situation, for example. The casual mention of a name. Or a place. How can I know what that trigger may be? And how can you? And if, in the unlikely event, that I should decide to open that window and look inside myself, should I take your hand?

Or should you take mine?

This story is based on the concept of Johari's Window – a tool used in therapy in order for the subject to recognise him or herself. The idea is to move as much as possible into the 'clear' window so that you have few secrets and are open and available. The Window was conceived by two men called John and Harry ...

THE CORNERS OF MY MIND

First published in the anthology 'Right Trusty and Well Beloved',
2019

"YOU NEVER WISHED to be queen, did you my love?" Richard squeezed his wife's hand gently. "Yet, t'was I who made you one, though it was never my intention to do so. How could I have anticipated the events that led to it? Yet here we are; I, Richard, third of that name, the King of England and you ... you my Queen."

Richard, perched on the edge of the large bed, stared at the ceiling of the small chamber. Beeswax candles were the only source of light, for the torch had long burned out and Richard had been of no mind to replace it. The moon, which should have been full and round, was dimmed red by the shadow of the night. A bad omen, men said, but of what they would make no comment.

"I loved you from the start, you know, Anne. Those childhood days at Middleham where we first met. I was thirteen, I recall it vividly. You nine, perhaps ten. As George, my brother, and I were put through our knightly training, you and Isabella would watch us, sitting on that low wall that was ever in danger of crumbling, laughing whenever we failed a tourney, clapping your hands with unashamed delight when we succeeded. You had such rosy cheeks then; your smile would spark the fire in them, I do swear! Such a pretty child you were, my dearest. Pretty and destined to grow into great beauty."

Richard rose to his feet, crossed to the unshuttered window, fiddling nervously with the ring on his little finger as he gazed out over the cobbled courtyard one storey below.

"I was devastated when Warwick fled and took you with him." He spoke to the eerily silent night. "Devastated, yes. But that was nothing to the fury I felt when the news came that he had married you to Edward of Westminster. Never mind that your father had betrayed my brother – nay, all England, truth be told – by allying himself to Marguerite, the French she-wolf; he had betrayed *me*. It had always been understood that we would be wed, just as George was to Isabella. No one escaped my anger; even Edward, my brother, avoided me though he still sought my counsel. And, as I have, with great shame, confessed to you, my dearest Anne, I found solace elsewhere."

Richard bit his lower lip, quelling the tears that threatened behind his eyes. He took a deep breath, holding it until it escaped as slowly as it had been drawn. He winced as the uncomfortable pull of hardened muscle aggravated his blighted shoulder. Then he shrugged. "I was young. Rejected – or so I felt." He turned his back on the bleak night but did not close the shutters. "You understood that, Anne, when I finally plucked up the courage to tell you. Yet you afforded nothing but kindness on John and Katherine, my bastards, when you did at last make their acquaintance. How relieved I was that you accepted them. They, too were grateful. Kate in especial. You were more of a mother to her than her own ever was."

A draught of air caused him to shiver. The candles briefly flared, sending dancing shadows across the wall hangings. Ensuring that he would not disturb her rest, Richard carefully resumed his place on the bed, taking hold once more of Anne's hand, stroking the back of it, tracing a finger along the lines of the dark blue veins that stood up from the thin skin above them. Such pretty, delicate hands, he thought. So soft. So gentle. So loving.

"I always tried to do the right thing, Anne. You believe me, don't you? I was never meant to be King, was never schooled for it. I always thought it would be father and then Edmund, but that was not to be. Instead it was Ned followed by George. Poor George!" He snorted a brief, low guffaw and then was silent for just a moment.

"I know how you disliked him, Anne, and I don't blame you for that for I well concur with your reasons. But it was never easy for him. Always overshadowed by Ned. George resented it, but Ned was always my hero. George wanted too much too quickly. Had he had an ounce of patience he would have been king today, not I. We had our differences, George and I, the most serious being his treatment of you, my dearest." Another deep, indrawn breath as he brushed his thumb delicately over the back of her hand. "I admit to being furious at that. How close did I come to killing him there in his own house where I searched for you in vain? Very close, I tell you. Very close indeed. And again, when you were finally found. I had begun to despair; I tell you true. Imagine my relief when the news came to me!" Richard carefully raised her hand, placed a tender kiss on the gold band that adorned her wedding finger, then released it from his grasp. Her fingers were cold. With tenderness he tucked the fur coverlet around her.

"There, that will keep you warmer," he said with a smile. "Yes, there were occasions when I could have killed George. Yet when Ned ordered me to inform him of that royal decision of execution, I could not do it." He released his breath through puffed cheeks, shook his head at the unwelcome return of memories. "We had the most ferocious argument that we had ever had, Ned and I. Ned would not be swayed and my cause was hopeless. And so, I did it. I told my George that Ned, our brother, our king, had decreed he must die. You should have seen his face, Anne. Even you would have taken pity on him. I recall I put my arm around him, though he shrugged it off and accused me of colluding with Ned I will never forget how white his face had turned. Surely no man should have to speak such words to his own brother?"

Richard buried his face in his hands, the memories a writhing viper striking at his brain. With thumb and forefinger, he pressed at the corner of his eyes, drew his grip down over his cheeks, his mouth and his chin, feeling the harsh rasp of new-grown beard-stubble on his skin.

"And ... and our son, our own-born Edward. Our dear, dear Edward. It hurts me still, Anne, as I know it does you. Mine enemies say that it was divine retribution, but Our Lord would not take such an action, I am sure. If it were I, or you, who had sinned, why would He take our child? My faith has never wavered despite everything. I believe that Edward was simply not strong enough to overcome the sicknesses that so frequently afflicted him. If that be God's will, then so be it. There was nothing either of us could do, Anne. You did so much to ease his pains. How much sleep did you lose, sitting by his bedside night after night? Whilst I was busy with affairs of the realm? Oh, but how I wish I could have taken your place, given you some respite from your trials. The day he was taken from us 'twas the worst of my life. The very worst. It will remain with me forever, when we dined alone at Nottingham and the messenger came with the dire news."

Richard bowed his head, suppressing a sob. *Too many sad times in my life, too many,* he thought. The deaths of his father and eldest brother, of George and Ned. Followed all too swiftly by his own son Edward. So cruel. So cruel!

Now only he was left. Richard. The last of the Plantagenet name. He sighed again. He even regretted the deaths of his enemies. Richard Neville, Anne's father the mighty earl of Warwick, basely slain by common soldiers and strictly against Ned's orders – though no doubt as king he would have ordered Warwick's execution had he been captured alive. Nor had Old

King Harry deserved to die. He had been harmless in himself, but while he had lived Marguerite would fight in his name. The poor man had barely known where he was when they had entered that cell in the Tower and extinguished his sad life. The memories trundled in like a parade of ghosts, he even felt sorry for the French woman. Not Buckingham, though. No, never Buckingham. Richard clenched his fists in anger. How he had trusted him, raised him up only to be repaid with betrayal and rebellion.

"There are many deaths on my conscience," Richard murmured; "Will Hastings, Thomas Vaughan, Richard Grey. Earl Rivers." He paused, other names, other faces prodding for his attention. He ignored them, swept their invasive presence aside. He raised his voice. "But not Buckingham. I have no regrets over his execution." He sat, staring at one of the tapestries adorning the wall, not seeing a single image that was depicted upon it. Not noticing that a draft was rippling it, making the silk features of men astride their horses, galloping through the woods in pursuit of a white stag, appear as if they really were moving.

"But they were necessary, Anne," he whispered. "Their deaths. There was no question that all of them were guilty of treason – 'twas all I could do! I know you advised me not to bestow that ultimate sentence, but I had no choice, my dearest. No choice at all. You do see that, do you not?"

Richard rose again, trembled as another gust of wind found its way through the window cracks and shivered through the room. "I should close the shutters," he said. "The physicians told me that the fresh air would aid you, but it grows too cold."

Nevertheless, he made no move to do so, merely stood staring into the night, said, "But I dwell on the dark side of my life, Anne. There were so many happy times. None happier than those days together at Middleham after our marriage. Those long rides on the moors; how free we were, how free we felt! Days of bliss indeed! And the sheer joy of our son after those years of trying." Richard chuckled. "Oh, we did try, Anne. We were both so desperate for a child of our own, Nevertheless I feared it would never happen, that we would not be so blessed. I know you suffered with the birth; I heard your cries from without. Lovell and I, we were in the chamber, outside, listening, praying. I paced the floor while Francis tried to calm me – most unsuccessfully, I do not hesitate to record – and then, then there was a silence and I was a-feared that something was wrong. But 'twas not so for there was another cry; a different one from the others. The cry of a new born babe! I have never told you this before, Anne, but Lovell and I, we danced! Yes! We embraced and we clutched our hands together and danced in wild circles all around that chamber such was our joy." He smiled, moved his feet in a brief, jigged homage to the memory of that euphoric moment.

"In spite of my impatience, I waited until the door of the birthing chamber opened and I was allowed in. Seeing you there, Anne, so pale, the sweat on your cheeks and brow but holding our little Edward, I do not think I have ever loved life – or you, my dear – more. Our son, our legitimate son and my heir. No man could have been prouder. You handed him to me, you recall? And I, I was reluctant take him for he was so small, so fragile, even bundled up as he was. I was so afraid I might crush him or worse, drop him! That was foolish and needless, of course, and I did take him and brushed his round, pink face with my finger. I was bursting with pride just then. I wanted to tell the world of my joy; let every man see *my* son, be that man a king or a peasant."

Floorboards creaked as he paced the room, he stopped beside another colourful embroidery that hung on the wall. Christ ascending to Heaven.

"Such a wondrous depiction," he murmured. "It comes to us all, Anne. Death. Death followed by Judgement. You, you will be judged favourably for I never knew of any act that you might have committed that would keep you from God's presence. But I? How will I be judged? As a man who did the best he could? Or as a man who committed foul deeds to achieve his ambitions?" He turned away, faced the bed. Fiddled once again with his finger ring. "I know what men say of me, but they are wrong. How will I be remembered, Anne? God knows the truth, but how will Man judge me? 'Tis not so much what a man does, my dearest, but how he is remembered, never mind the truths of his life." Richard sighed a deep, regretful sigh. "But that is for contemplation at another time, another day, another month. Another year."

He returned to the bed and once more took Anne's hand in his. Lost in his thoughts, he did not hear the door open, nor Lovell's footsteps. Not until he felt a hand on his shoulder did he look up at Lovell's grim face.

"My Lord," Lovell said. Then, almost as a whisper, "Richard. She has gone. It is over. Let the women enter and tend her, prepare her body for her meeting with God."

Richard, the king, the most powerful man in the realm of all England looked, blank, at his friend. Said, after a moment, "How am I to live without her, Francis? How?"

DEATH OF A HIGHWAYMAN

EVEN ON A COLD APRIL MIDDAY, Tyburn was always a great attraction on a hanging day. The more so when a notorious highwayman was amongst those condemned.

Richard Foster smiled and nodded his head at the crowd that lined the filthy streets. Most just pointed at him, some waved back and a very few threw rotten fruit at him. Despite the cords that bound his wrists in front of him, he contrived to catch a bruised apple, take a bite and propel the fruit back into the crowd. This brought a cheer and he smiled. He sat down on his own coffin and looked up at the sky above. *A grey day in all respects,* he thought.

Ahead of him six other carts formed the procession; five of them contained men guilty of various crimes and the other a woman who had robbed her own father. Seven wasn't a large number for the crowds to enjoy, yet there were traders selling baked potatoes and pies, ale and fruit. They, like the pickpockets and prostitutes, would at least make a profit this day.

Although it was not that far from Newgate Gaol to Tyburn village, the journey had already taken three hours. The first stop had been at St Sepulchre's Church where the bellman entreated the small crowd there to pray for the souls of the condemned. Two further stops were made where the prisoners were allowed a last drink. Foster had taken his time. No need to rush anything today.

Now, coming closer with every step of the horse, he could see the triangular shape of the Tyburn tree. The Nevergreen Tree, they called it. The only type of tree that bears fruit more than once a year.

It had been a short walk through life from cradle to gallows for Dick Foster. He'd had a good upbringing, was educated. A goodly inheritance awaited him. When civil war broke out he'd backed the king. But with Charles' defeat, Foster lost everything. The stately home, the promised fortune – all gone. The woman he loved. Snatched away too. What choices had he had? Penniless and outlawed, The Road was the only way to survive.

Highwaymen were commonplace, so many of them in the same straits as Foster. Rob to survive. It took guts to stop a coach on your own. But a nice brace of pistols helped. Coachmen had no desire to be shot any more than the rich inhabitants of the coaches they guided across the lonely areas of heath or common.

Foster had no qualms about taking a lady's jewels or a merchant's purse. He was not averse to striking either if they refused to give up their booty. Aye, he'd killed, too. A stupid, fat businessman who swore on the life of his wife – sitting horrified beside him – that he carried no coin. But the fool had reached for a pistol and Foster discharged his piece into the man's face.

No, Foster had been no angel despite his reputation of being 'The Laughing Highwayman'. As he had been. Most of the time. If his victims gave up their valuables without fuss then he would treat the gentlemen to a ribald joke, or the ladies with a kiss on the hand before sending them on their way.

He watched as the preceding carts were backed up and aligned, the prisoners told to stand while a halter was placed over each of their bare heads. Nooses tightened around their necks. Fresh, new hemp. Later, the hangman would cut each length of rope, cut them into even pieces and sell them. The rope that hanged Dick Foster would fetch a fair price indeed. The woman and one of the men voided themselves and were roundly booed. And then, at the signal from the hangman, the horses bounded forward, the boards of the carts slid away from the condemned's feet and six bodies jerked and kicked and swung wildly in the air. Some people rushed forward, pulling hard on the legs of one of the choking men and snapped his neck, saving him further agony. The rest struggled in vain, legs kicking the air until all were still save for a gentle, almost peaceful swaying. The last one had taken almost a quarter of the hour to finally expire.

"On your feet, Foster," a voice barked.

Foster rose. For a moment his legs wobbled but he soon regained composure. *The effects of the rickety cart*, he told himself.

Such a well-known name as Dick Foster afforded the honour of being raised above the crowds in order that all could see him die – even those at the back of the crowd. Waiting on him: the hangman, the noose dangling loose from one of the triple arms of the Tree, a stool upon which Foster would stand.

With a surprisingly steady tread Foster climbed the steps of the gallows. He nodded to the hangman; there were niceties to be observed. Traditions such as dressing in his best clothes, which Foster had done so earlier that morning when the irons had been struck off back at Newgate. His clothes, and indeed his body, would become the property of the hangman who would make a tidy profit from their selling. He asked for the rope binding his wrists to be severed so that he may remove his coat. The hangman hesitated. Was this some trick? A plan to escape?

"I would remove it so that the people may see I do not quake with fear. And that I may personally hand it to you," Dick added with a charming smile. Hoped that it was a warm enough day for him not to shiver with cold, lest he give a wrong impression.

The hangman grunted, unbound the rope.

The Highwayman smiled again, removed the coat.

The smile remained in place while the rope was rebound.

Dick shrugged, ah well a forlorn hope of an escape had been worth a try.

The hangman took the coat and actually smiled back at the condemned man. "You have a speech?"

"I do. With your permission. Oh, and you may find a coin or two in those pockets," Foster added in a stage whisper accompanied with a sly wink. The exchange was noted, those that heard the words clearly, applauded.

He stood firmly on the tail of the cart, dressed now in a clean shirt of fine linen, neatly embroidered around the collar. His breeches were of doe skin and the boots were of high-quality leather and polished to a shine.

Forcing a broad smile onto his face he scanned the crowd, most waiting in anticipated silence. "A goodly gathering," he began, "I thank you my friends for attending me this ... this auspicious day!" There were some muted cheers. Unperturbed, Foster continued. "My first duty is to entreat you all not to follow my wicked example else you will find yourselves exactly where I find myself now. For a sinner I have been and a sinner I will ... die." The first wavering. Confession was always good whether it was sincere or not. The crowds almost demanded it. Without one they would pelt the victim once more with anything that came to hand. All Foster had now was to please the crowd and perhaps gain a place in folklore. Foster drew in a deep breath, one that was so close to his last. There was to be no dramatic rescue; it had always been a vain hope. "Trust in the Lord and heed the words of the Gospels: good advice, I must add, for I wish I had done so. But before I pay with my life for the crimes I have committed and for which I have been rightly condemned, I beg one request: you, sir, you with the fiddle: pray strike up a lively tune, for I have always loved to dance!"

This brought laughter and clapping; oh how the crowd loved a bold speech, well spoken and made with humour.

The fiddler began to play. A jig. What else? Satisfied, Foster spoke softly now. "Do your duty, Master hangman."

He climbed onto the stool, felt the halter tighten around his neck, chafing the skin. The stool beneath his feet gave way and his legs kicked empty air but could find no purchase ...

A MURDER OF AUTHORS

"WELCOME, LADIES ... AND GENTLEMAN," Alice St Jean began with an acknowledging nod towards Monty Donaldson, the only male present in the seated circle of females. "Christine sends her apologies – one of her children is feeling a bit poorly. First though, may I introduce our new member, Diana Bennett. Would you like to introduce yourself, Diana?"

Diana looked around the circle, noting the staccato hand clapping and warm, friendly, encouraging smiles. With the middle finger of her right hand, she pushed her spectacles back up her nose. "Thank you for having me here," she began nervously. "I'm not really a writer ..."

"Nonsense!" interjected Angela Knight. "You write, therefore you are!"

"Hear, hear," supported Alice.

"Well," Diana stumbled, "yes, I suppose so. But I have not had anything published, unlike yourselves. Anyway, I've always enjoyed writing stories and thought I'd try a full-length novel."

"Is it a crime novel?" Monty asked. "That is the genre for all of us here."

"Oh yes," Diana responded. "A murder mystery."

"Would you like to tell us something about it?" This from Denise Darke, a large woman in all aspects.

"Ok. The basic plot is of a woman who is abused and humiliated by her husband. She's a bit of an introvert but it suddenly becomes all too much for her and well, she murders him. I feel I need a little help with some of the finer details."

"Such as?" Alice asked, inclining her head to one side.

"Er, police procedures for one. And how to dispose of the body for another. She is rather naive and the act happened rather suddenly and, well, there she is, alone in the house with a dead body on her hands."

Alice smiled. "Well, our expert on police matters here is Sally: her Inspector Dover books are very popular and," Alice hid her face behind her hand and said in a stage whisper "there is talk of a TV mini series!"

"Oh, stop it," Sally laughed. "You know that nothing has yet been decided. I'm on tenterhooks, of course. But," she turned her attention back to Diana, "it depends upon what era you are talking about. Mine are set in the modern day so I'm pretty up to date with current procedures. I have contacts, you know!" She tapped the side of her nose with her index finger."

"Yes," Diana said. "It is set in the modern day."

"Angela," said Alice, "how do you get rid of your bodies?"

Angela, mid-fifties, bobbed blonde hair, laughed. "I do hope you don't mean that literally, Alice!" Everybody laughed, including Diana. "Of course there are a number of ways, but it also depends of the circumstances. Was there any blood and if so, how much? Where was the murder committed? At home? On holiday? Well, you did say in the house, so I presume it is their house. Would your protagonist be able to move the body? I mean, does the heroine have a disability? Is she a small woman and he perhaps a large man? I would not recommend burying the body under the patio or in a shallow grave in a spot crawling with regular dog walkers. Boiling the bodies or dissolving in acid is not a good idea – that's how Dennis Nilson got caught. The stench alerted the neighbours."

"I remember that," Diana nodded in agreement, pulling a face. "And Fred and Rose West, of course."

Many nods in agreement.

"Let me have a little think and perhaps we'll talk when we have a break." Angela mused.

"Thank you, yes, I'd like that.

"Right:" Alice took charge. "Let's move on. Monty: I believe you have a new chapter to read to us?"

"If you ladies don't mind," Monty beamed. "For a bit of background, Diana, I write about a character called Marty Diamond. He's a gumshoe – a private eye in New York City just before the Second World War. Well," Donaldson exuded superciliousness in the extreme, "during it, actually, if we accept that the Yanks weren't in there at the start!"

Diana listened, but nor for long. The style was hackneyed, the main character a stereotype, the situation, to her untrained mind, implausible. She soon ceased to hear the words. Her eyelids began to drop and she fought to keep them from closing. The Church Hall was warm even as the summer evening began to take over. There was no breeze coming through the half open windows. Diana looked around, her gaze alighting on the table covered with a white cloth. Cups, saucers, sugar and the ingredients for an adequate refreshment.

"*And,*" Monty seemed to be reaching a conclusion, "*when I opened the door to my apartment, I was face to face with an old enemy. And he was holding a gun.*"

"Oh Bravo, Monty," applauded Alice. "Leaving us in suspense yet again!"

Diana joined in the light applause and then rose with the others as Alice announced refreshments. "Let's grab a coffee and go outside," Angela whispered, "I'm dying for a smoke."

Outside, Angela glanced back at the door. "God, he's awful!

Claims he's the only man in England who can write American thrillers. He's right there: no one would want to of course, not like that! Cigarette?"

Diana giggled, then nodded. "I don't normally, but I've had a day of it today and I think I really could do with one. Thank you."

Angela blew smoke out and said, "So: your problem. How are we going to get rid of the body?"

Diana sighed. "I haven't made my mind up yet. But I will certainly take your suggestions on board."

"It's more than that. Your protagonist – what is her name?"

"Mary."

"Mary. Well now: you say the act was sudden, possibly even an accident? I mean, she didn't intend to kill him, after all. Of course, the sensible thing to do would be to go to the police straight away, but then you wouldn't have much of a plot, would you!" Angela laughed.

"No, that's right. Besides, she's frightened. No one must know that a murder has been committed."

"Depending on the method, that may not be too much of a worry. But the police are very good and they are sure to find the body sooner or later. DNA and Forensics are pretty damned accurate these days."

Diana's coffee had cooled so she sipped at it in between nervous puffs on the cigarette. "Oh, I don't want the body to be found. At all."

"Aha, so Mary gets away with it?"

"Absolutely. I think she deserves the freedom."

Angela looked at her, then smiled. "You go, girl. Girl Power, eh!"

"Something like that," Diana laughed.

The second half of the meeting was a little more interesting with a lively discussion about what made good names for characters or, more importantly, bad names. Diana joined in, laughing at some of the more humorous suggestions.

She declined the later offer to join them for a drink in the Red Lion across the road. As she drove the short distance home, she had a more positive plot line in her head.

She clicked open the automatic garage door and drove carefully in, getting as close to George's car as she could without bumping into it. Then she exited the garage, locked the door and let herself in. The lights were off and she cursed as she tripped over the foot of her dead husband.

THE GHOST OF WHITE HART LANE

THEY CALLED HIM 'THE GHOST'. He had that amazing ability to drift unnoticed into spaces on the pitch which the opposition had not covered. From there he either scored or laid on a telling pass. He was my idol.

I came up through the usual levels; school team, then representing my district and county and was on the brink of selection for the National team in a schoolboy International against Scotland at Wembley. An annoying, stupid injury shattered that dream and the chance never came again for it had been the last fixture of the season.

I received the letter during the summer holidays. Spurs had been scouting me, it appeared, and offered me a trial in August. Over the Moon? I showed that letter to everyone I met. "I'm going to play for Spurs," I boasted without thought about how long that would take or the thought that it might not actually happen.

Football then was not the glamorous life that it is today: Cliff Jones had a butcher's shop on Tottenham High Road and, allegedly, would do a morning's work on a Saturday and then walk down to the ground in time for the afternoon's match. If Spurs were at home, obviously.

I did well in the trial and was offered a schoolboy contract.

Whether money passed between club and my Dad, I never found out. It was common in those days. If any did, I didn't see any of it.

My first job at Spurs? Cleaning John White's boots. I'll never forget the first time I handed them to him, sparkling with Dubbin. He looked at them, frowned and said, "Ye missed a bit, laddie." I felt the heat rise in my cheeks, grabbed them out of his hands and inspected them. I looked up at him in bewilderment and was met by that toothy grin of his. "Only joking, son," he said mischievously, "they're fine."

I had to attend night school and take an apprenticeship in carpentry. It was policy: few schoolboys actually achieved their dream and the club insisted that they had a trade to fall back on. Training consisted largely of sweeping the terraces and then spending a lot of time just running up and down the steps. Games were few and far between, but after a couple of seasons I made it in to the reserve team.

In 1961, Spurs won the Double – FA Cup and 1st Division in the same season. Only the third club in history to achieve that and the first one in that century. Instrumental in that magnificent season was John White. By that time I was playing regularly on a Saturday morning on the ground where I had witnessed so many first team matches. I scored a few goals for the reserves and, in my mind, was knocking on the door for my first team debut. But, of course, in the days before substitutes, that meant waiting for someone to be injured or at least suffer a dramatic loss of form.

My chance came one cold Saturday in January. The injured player? John White. Bitter sweet then. I sat in the dressing room surrounded by some of the biggest names in football, shivering. Cold? No, I was just in awe. John White was in the dressing room, chatting to the players and then he drew me aside.

"Play your game, son," he told me. "Ye've an intelligent head on your shoulders. Time your runs, hit your passes true and if you get your chances, have a go. Don't be afraid of the opposition and don't be afraid of your teammates. Express yourself out there and all will be well."

Trotting out near the back of the line, the welcoming cheers of the crowd hit me like a brick wall. I'd stood in the stands many times and contributed to that noise, but this was different. For a moment I felt sick, but once I'd touched the ball in the pre-match kickabout, all that disappeared.

My introduction to Fist Division football was an unceremonious shove in the back and I was sent sprawling in the mud. But I had a half decent game. Two shots, one well wide and the other forcing a good save by the 'keeper that gave us a corner. Got in a few tackles and made some good passes. Indeed, I laid the ball out to Cliff Jones whose cross was headed in by Bobby Smith for the only goal of the game. Jones came up to me and ruffled my hair. "Good ball, boyo," he grinned. I really felt as if I had arrived.

In truth, my 'glorious career' didn't develop. I only managed a couple more games that season, neither of them particularly memorable. And when all others were negotiating new contracts, I was called to see the Boss, Bill Nicholson, and was told, with genuine regret that he was going to accept an offer from Leyton Orient for my services.

My world fell apart then. I agreed to talk to the club and eventually did sign for them. A week later I collected my things and made my way out of White Hart Lane. *I'll be back*, I vowed to myself. I bumped into John White on my way out. He either guessed or knew why I was looking so distraught. In truth, I was almost in tears.

He put his hand on my shoulder. "Life can be hard sometimes," he began. "Ups and downs, ye ken? One door closes and all that. Ye have to take it in your stride, son. Trust me. Ye'll bounce back, ye'll see. Just apply ye'sel' an' ye'll have a good career." He patted me in a companionable manner on the shoulder and made for his car. Then he turned and called back. "Ye take o' ye'sel' and I'll see ye around, yeah?"

He was wrong. Neither of us knew than that we would never meet again.

I didn't do too badly at Orient, becoming a crowd favourite. The following summer I was on holiday in Scotland when the news came through: John White had died, struck by lightning on a golf course in Enfield. I sat and sobbed for the rest of the day.

My career was fading. Five years at Orient and then another two at Peterborough United. During the second of those we reached the last sixteen of the League Cup and were drawn away to ... Tottenham Hotspur!

At least I'd been able to fulfil one promise in my life. I had returned to White Hart Lane. A coach took us from the Midlands to North London. I stepped down from the vehicle and just looked around me. Nothing had changed. I drunk in the atmosphere. When I trotted onto the pitch I felt that at least some of the crowd were welcoming me back.

We lost one-nil. Jimmy Greaves got the winner a little after half time. I wasn't quite as devastated as perhaps I should have been. I limped out into the car park; I'd got a knock during the game which ultimately would end my career. But I didn't know that then either.

It was dark, late in October and a chilly wind swept away the sweet wrappers and other after match detritus.

"Ye ken, things needn't be too bad. Ye have a good head on ye an' ye know the game. Wouldn't surprise me if ye made a decent manager yet."

I turned, the hairs on my arms tingling with anticipation ...

There was no one in sight. Yet I had heard the words as clear as day. They weren't just in my head, they were real.

And I knew who had spoken them too. The Ghost of White Hart Lane.

THE STONES AT ROLLRIGHT

HER NAME WAS RHIANNON. She told me this quite freely after I had made a gentle enquiry as to why she was digging small holes in the ground.

From her kneeling position she looked up at me, her corn-flower blue eyes sparking in the afternoon sunlight. "The crystals," she explained. "they came from the earth and back to the earth they should go." She showed me the palm of her hand, darkened with fresh dirt, revealing a half dozen or so perfectly smooth and brightly coloured stones. She dropped them into the hole and covered it over. Then she stood, wiping her hands on her long, flowing skirt. "They replenish each other," she told me.

I won't say she was the prettiest girl I had ever seen, but far from the ugliest. Her attraction was the innocence that surrounded her like a halo. Blonde hair hung well below her shoulders, kept tidy by a braided circlet tied lightly with a lemon coloured ribbon at the back of her head. It added to the fragile, fey look that she had.

"Have you been here before?"

I shook my head.

"Do you know the story of the Stones?"

"No. I didn't know they had one. I suppose I just assumed that they grew here naturally. If you see what I mean. Tell the truth, I didn't know they were even here. I'm heading for Banbury, fancied the pretty route and stopped at the Garden Centre where the waitress told me about them."

Rhiannon gave me the smile a wise mother gives to a misinformed or particularly stupid child. "Sit with me, if you will, and I will tell you."

Being in no hurry, I did as I was told and sat cross-legged on the grass while she remained on her knees. Just like a child in class, I hugged my thighs. Her friendliness was disarming yet reassuring: she had no fear of me and knew that she had no cause to.

"Some say they are magical stones placed here by giants or gods. But the best story is that they were all once men, turned to stone by a great witch. They also say that it is impossible to count the number of them, for each time you try, you're sure to get a different answer."

"Really?" I turned my head, noted the numbers and rechecked. I must have miscounted for the tally was different, but I shook my head. Rhiannon grinned knowingly. My return grin was rather sheepish. "And all turned to stone by a witch?"

She nodded easily and happily. "So the story goes." She paused momentarily before continuing. "There was a great king, victorious in battle, camped on the hill here when he and his men were visited by the witch. She begged food of them and they gave her some, but reluctantly. Mischievously and mindful of this king's boastfulness, she offered him a wager: if he could cross the top of the hill in but seven strides and see the village of Long Compton beyond, he would become High King of all England." Again, a reflective pause. "Well, my friend, the men that were with him thought it all madness and begged him to refuse the wager, but he ignored them because he was a bold and confident man and the task should prove an easy one for him. He took his place and measured his seven strides without effort, whilst his men stood apart, whispering amongst themselves, for they now recognised his arrogance and madness."

I waited for more. It was not forthcoming. "And did he become king of all England?" I asked eventually.

Rhiannon shook her head and laughed. "Of course not! This was a witch he was dealing with, remember? And no man should attempt to outwit a witch." Her face creased into something close to a frown, "Just as he was about to take his seventh step, she caused a new hill to rise up from the ground and obscure the view so that he was unable to see the village. '*As Long Compton thou canst not see, king of England thou shalt not be*,' Rhiannon quoted. "She turned them all to stone, he standing there," she pointed and I followed her gaze to the single stone surrounded by a protective iron fence. "Alone atop the hill while his men were petrified in a circle nearby. They call those stones The Whispering Knights." Her fingers pointed to the relevant stones.

"And what became of the witch?" I asked.

She gazed up at the sky reflectively. "They do say that she turned herself into an elder tree. Why? I have no idea! Perhaps she had used up all her spells? Or powers? Do you believe in such things?"

I hesitated. "In witches? Well, I don't know, to be honest. Certainly people used to believe in them. I mean, Salem and Pendle and all that."

That clear sky seemed to cloud over as I spoke. Rhiannon shook her head as if to clear the darkness and the sun shone again from her eyes.

"Permit me to give you a tip: be kind to witches for the rewards will come. But be unkind to them and they will find their revenge one day."

"I will remember that. Thank you," I said, nodding wisely.

She rose to her feet. A fresh breeze ruffled the short sleeves of her peasant style top. "I should go," she said, smiling as ever, offering her hand for me to shake. Nothing else. "Thank you for spending some time with me."

"My car is quite close by," I stammered, "can I – may I – give you a lift?"

"That's very kind, but no, thank you."

She turned her back and ambled away to the top of the hill and disappeared below the brow. I followed and watched her go. Heading for the shade of an elder tree.

THE FLYING MONK

In this tale, set in the England of 1015,
Torr is the leader of a troop of men in loyal service to Edmund
'Ironside' Ætheling, son of Æthelred II.

FIRES CRACKLED in the silence of the night as Torr approached his men. He joined them and sat cross-legged on the ground. He knew the men were restless after days of inactivity: at least he had something to tell them.

"We'll be on the move come morning, lads," he announced.

"About bloody time," someone muttered.

"Where to this time?" Eofwic, Torr's second in command asked.

Torr scratched the back of his neck. "West," he replied. "Place called Malmesbury."

"Nice there," someone said. This was Cenhelm. Torr thought he'd been asleep, but apparently not.

"'Been there, have you?" asked Ryce sarcastically. Ryce rarely spoke at all: Torr guessed he was bored. He liked the big man. Short but heavily muscled, he was a formidable opponent.

"Oh, yes, indeed," Cenhelm, wiping sweat from his brow. "You never know, we might get to meet Brother Eilmer." Cenhelm was a grizzled old soldier, full of stories of his experiences. Torr sensed that another tall tale was about to be told.

"And who be he?" Renfred asked innocently

Cenhelm turned to face him. "You've not heard of Eilmer lad?"

"I wouldn't have asked else, would I?"

Cenhelm nodded. That sounded reasonable to him. "Well then, I will tell you: Eilmer is the man who flew."

"What?" Eorfwic cried in amazement, spluttering out the water he had been drinking.

"The man who flew, I tell you."

From the back, Ryce grunted.

Torr sighed. "Go on then, tell us."

"I'm about to, ain't I?" Cenhelm pulled himself to a sitting position. "Well,'twere about five year past now," Cenhelm continued, unperturbed by the merriment he had caused. "This Eilmer, he's a brother at the monastery at Malmesbury – Benedictine or some such, and he's right clever, he is. Knows all about stars and things. Said he'd seen a great hairy star in the skies when he was about six years old and reckoned it was a bad sign. Danes came a-raiding the very next year." Cenhelm paused for a heartbeat. "Well, that's by the by." He coughed and spat onto the ground. "Right; so Eilmer told me he'd been studyin' the birds, wonderin' how they managed to fly and wouldn't it jus' be wonderful if he could be like them? So he has this idea to build himself some wings – chicken feathers on some sort of frame – which he ties to his arms and his feet and up he goes to the top of the Abbey tower and there he waits for the right wind and throws himself off."

"And what happened to him?" Torr asked, laughing.

"Giss a chance! Off the tower he goes, catches the wind, flaps his arms and legs like a big brown bird and, I'm telling you true, he flies through the air. About a furlong, they reckoned, right over the

Abbey walls an' out into the fields before his strength ran out an' he started fallin' out o' the sky." Again, Cenhelm paused. "Came down with a hell of a thump. Didn't kill 'im. Broke both his legs, though."

That dissolved the company into laughter.

"S'alright for you to laugh," Cenhelm protested. "If he's still there, you can ask him yoursel's. He'll be happy to tell you. You can't miss him; short, skinny fellow. Walks with a limp," he added.

❧

Malmesbury stood upon the top of a hill in the range known as Cotswold. The rivers Avon and Ingleburn wove their way around the town, carefully avoiding each other until the time that they converged just to the south of the town. Malmesbury Abbey stood in the centre of all this, a dutiful mother keeping a watchful eye over her children.

"Don't say much, do they?" observed Torr to Cenhelm as the men were escorted to the refectory.

"Not a lot, no," replied the soldier. "They can do. I mean, they don't have no strict vows o' silence like some other orders, but speaking is rather limited nonetheless. Not much to talk about I suppose, what with all that prayin' and singin' at all times o'day and night."

Inside they were shown to a table and served with small bowls of porridge and of fish soup, hastily prepared and not fully heated. But it was better than nothing to the hungry men. Cenhelm was seated opposite Torr and he looked up as a voice from behind his leader said, "I know you. Let me see – no, don't tell me – Cenhelm! That's it, isn't it? Cenhelm. Well, well, well! How are you keeping, old friend?"

Cenhelm's face broke into a broad grin. "Brother Eilmer! Good to see you looking well! Done any flyin' lately?"

All of Torr's company were attentive now – had this man

really flown? Was Cenhelm's tale a true one after all? Torr turned and looked up, surprised by what he saw. He had imagined Eilmer to be an older man, probably short on wit, but this man was little more than twenty years of age – certainly a few years away from his thirties – lean as a stick, with short flaxen hair shaven on top to show a bald pate.

"Ah, sadly, no," Eilmer sighed. "Old Abbot Ælfric died that same year and my lord Abbot Æthelweard has strictly forbidden me any further attempts."

"Ah, 'tis true then, the tale that Cenhelm has spun us?" Eorfwic blurted out.

Eilmer nodded. "Aye, that it is, young sir." He smiled ruefully to himself at the memory. "It could have been a better attempt had I not been so impatient and taken the time to fashion. myself a proper tail to stabilise the flight. But, there we are. The impetuosity of youth, eh? Now, if you will excuse me."

It was all Torr could do to stop himself from laughing.

THE DIAMOND

by Barbara Gaskell Denvil
Originally written for Discovering Diamonds
In December 2017

Late 15th Century London

I WALKED SLOWLY, enjoying the soft splatters of rain on my back and the gentle music of its fall. It trickled from my hair to my shoulders, and down from my shoulders to my breasts and the little damp chill made me feel more alive. In the past I would not have been able to wear my hair loose. A married woman does not parade her hair in the sight of God. But now I do as I wish, and my hair is a curling drip of blonde ringlets. It feels free and I like it.

The path was deeply shadowed, which spun its own patterns from twisted tree trunks and sudden fences, to hay barns, ditches and the flickers of a star through the clouds. Midnight. The hour for hauntings. I decided that was quite amusing.

By the morning I had arrived at the gates of London as they were unlocked, and slipped through behind the usual barge of monks off to earn their crusts, goose-boys shepherding their flat tar-footed flock, marketeers with their barrows of fresh fruit and busy housewives, eager to be first in the shopping queues. The rain, never heavy, was no more than a silver mist and a pale sun oozed from between the cloud cover. I hurried east and took the back streets into the deeper shadows of the Tower. Here, ramshackle and smelling of depression, stood the old tenements but I travelled deeper into Fish Street. It's where I used to live.

The street could be noisy, almost bilious on a Friday morning when everyone with half an appetite came to buy whatever had been freshly caught. And then again in the evening as they piled into the tavern at the slope of the Bridge to puke back the ale that had accompanied it. But my husband had not been a noisy man. He was sitting now in the downstairs solar, hands clasped sadly over his chest, eyes closed, no doubt contemplating his long-lost wife, or perhaps just the discourses of Plato, the benefits of King Richard III over those of King Edward IV, or the alternative. Or possibly what he would tell the maid to cook for dinner. It wasn't Friday, I had seen to that.

He didn't see me, poor Alfred. Eyes firmly shut against the intrusion of real life, he dozed or dreamed, or both. There were no noticeable improvements to our house, nor any new comforts or furnishings. He wore, as he always had, a drab brown broadcloth doublet with a peplum to his knees over black woollen hose which wrinkled around the ankles. His shirt peeped at the neck, creased white ribbons barely tied. He wore no rings. His hair would have been in his eyes, had they been open. But his expression was benign, perhaps peaceful. It is possible that since losing his wife, life seemed to him more amenable. I couldn't blame him. I had always been a rather tumble-down skirts-up sort of wife, wanting more than he could be bothered giving, and chattering about things he considered banal.

No. There was no possibility at all that my poor sweet husband had stolen my diamond.

I left the house, but first I scratched a kiss and the shape of a heart on the old beaten top of his little work-table. He would know that was me. He wouldn't understand, but he'd smile.

From there I walked over the Bridge. It was alight with business and bawds, balderdash, dogs barking and donkeys braying. I pushed through, avoided the inevitable squash in the centre where those travelling north from Southwark refused to give way to those from central London travelling south, and hurried through London's southern gate. No traitors' heads were spiked over the gate today. The sunshine had replaced the mizzle and was warming. The clouds had blown away.

Southwark plunged me back into shadows. Streets too narrow, tenements too close together, taverns and lodging inns built too tall so that the upper storeys bent over as though spying, and only the bishop's palace looking worth the trouble of a visit. But it was the thieves' dens I was intending to visit and, naturally, I knew just where they were.

The three better known, and the one less known, were crowded into the alley that pretended to overlook the Thames, the alley as crooked as the shop-owners, and I started with Piping Pete's. He was busy with a customer. Listening to every word, I managed to sneak into the corner, and rummaged in the chests and boxes. Piping Pete was tall, skinny, cross-eyed and had a nose like a long tin whistle. But he didn't have my diamond. I moved on to Barnacle Doggy. He didn't have my diamond either. The largest shop of dealing and destruction was the Palace of Gaiety, which dealt in many things. It took a very long time to search that place, with nearly sixteen prostitutes sleeping there (the sixteenth was Ned, who didn't really count) but not one single sparkle of diamond was either hidden or on show. I found a small ruby, which I was quite sure had been filched and couldn't possibly belong to Dim-witted Dorothy, but it wasn't my business and I left it there.

The nastiest little lair was in the cellar of a tavern, half dug by hand, and here lived Edward O'Cleaf. Thief, murderer, traitor and bastard, but strangely a man with an ingenious sense of humour. While he made his audience chuckle and roar, he stole everything they had on them.

He was out and I was exceedingly glad. I managed to creep in, and searched his hole from top to bottom. No diamonds. Ignoring the completely fraudulent letters entitling him to positions of legal authority and the few genuine letters proving various lord's treachery and infidelity, I found no jewellery of any kind.

So, I flitted through the Southwark taverns where a few of the less enterprising did private deals, and still found nothing. I wandered all the way back over the Bridge, along Little Thames Street, up past St. Paul's and into Goldsmith's Row. Here the wealthy shop owners opened their shutters each morning, lifted them down and laid them out to make a counter facing the street. There they stood, beaming at the passing crowds, ready to sell at the highest possible price, some of the most beautiful wares in Europe. It was the cleanest street in London and here no one ever dared empty their chamber pot into the gutters. The shelves beamed with glory. There were pewter, silver and golden goblets. There were even some in the new Murano crystal, which few could afford. Gold shimmered from shelves, huge crafted bowls of silver, silk drapery with tassels held in silver bands, and necklaces, rings and broaches of patterned and encrusted gold.

Here was the assortment of shops which might sell such a valuable object as a diamond ring. Only if they considered it legal merchandise, but perhaps, without me dancing up a scene, the legality of such a sale would seem as irrefutable.

Customers were welcome. I entered every shop. Only one had a diamond for sale. Smaller and less elaborate than my stolen prize, it was a broach, pretty and almost as rare as my own, but not my own. My own beautiful ring was nowhere. I was disappointed. Without climbing into the bedchamber of every wealthy lady in the land, or pick the lock of every coffer, what else could I do to discover my diamond?

Disconsolate, I wandered back to Fish Street. Most shops were now closed for dinner time and most customers had scuttled off to cook and to eat. I crept back into the shadows to see if my husband was eating roast venison, bought with the wealth my diamond could have brought him. Instead, he was now sitting in the window seat, watching those few who still wandered the sun-reflecting cobbles. Last night's rain had not yet dried entirely, and the trickles between cobbles, the sheen on the thatches, the glow on the window mullions and the puddles on the doorsteps threw the pretty spangled sunshine back in its cheerful face. I peeped in the window but withdrew at once, for that was where Alfred sat.

He had been crying. I choked, wanting to cry myself, seeing him like that. He had streaks down each side of his face and his eyes were pink and puffy. His hands were tightly knuckled against his stomach, bulging where my good cooking and his middle-age had spread it over his narrow belt. He hadn't been the best husband in the world. I hadn't been the best wife. Of course, he never knew about my disreputable past, but I had tried to make him happy. Perhaps sometimes I had succeeded. Had he really been crying over me? Perhaps it had simply been a headache or the first signs of diarrhoea after too many oysters. His brother might have punched him again, as he had a year ago when I marched over to brother Godwin's larger house and thrown a bowl of scalding cabbage broth in his face.

I had shouted, "How dare you punch my husband!"

And the stupid man had replied, "Because he irritates me and always thinks he's right and I am wrong." He had glared, pointing a long knotty finger right into my face. "I say we have no right to read the Holy Bible in a language we understand. Had God intended us to understand, He'd have written it in English. Instead He wrote in Latin. We should not meddle with the scriptures. My wicked brother speaks heresy. He's lucky I only punched him. If you want to read that stuff, learn Latin, I yelled at

Alfred. And you should learn common decency and common sense, he yelled back. So I hit him."

That's when I threw the soup. It had come off the boil by then and just left a few colourful scorch marks which improved his looks no end.

My diamond was huge. Nearly as large as my little finger nail, and as white as white can be. Sparkling, gleaming, spangled and stunning. It was square cut, and a tiny pearl gripped each corner, Gems I adored. It was set on a plain gold circlet which just fitted my finger, and had been given to me by my mother on her deathbed. It was very special to me for several reasons.

I was coming back from the wash-house when it was stolen, just about a month ago. I had a huge basket of damp shirts, sheets, shifts and other linens under my arm, and was about to hurry into my own doorway, ready to spread these in the kitchen to dry by the fire. Someone crept up behind me. I never saw him, but he hit me over the head with a hammer and I dropped my basket. All those things I'd spent ages boiling and scrubbing were strewn across the street, and I was on my knees. With my head screaming in pain. Probably my skull was cracked. Well, my head had never been my strongest part. It certainly hurt.

Then he twisted my arm up behind my back, grabbed the ring finger, and tried to pull the diamond off, the pea-brained fool. I always wore it, simply because it was too tight to move. So my attacker cut my finger right off, still wearing the ring.

Now I was thinking of something else. It gave me an idea.

Alfred's brother Godwin lived in the next street. I ran around the corner and I went to his house. Unlocked, easy enough to sneak in, up those old wooden stairs, into each separate room. No diamond hidden in his bedchamber, nothing in any coffer, nor cupboard, not under the bed and certainly not on view. He didn't have a kitchen. There weren't many places to look. I went into the downstairs solar and watched the lump of a man snoring on the settle, mouth wide open, small squint eyes shut, both nose and mouth dribbling. I searched the room.

Then I thought of the most obvious place. I managed to untie his purse from his belt without waking him, emptied it onto the floor. The tiny clank of coins rattled, and out rolled my diamond ring. There it was, as shining and gorgeous as it had been when I wore it. My beloved ring. No mangled flesh, no blood, no skin or other remains of my finger. It had been cleaned and now it shone with pride. I picked it up and kissed it. My mother had given it to me and the man she had loved so much had given it to her. But I couldn't put it on now. I turned, wondering what to do. Then I knew. I walked over and poked it hard down into Godwin's ugly gaping throat. I pushed it so far that he immediately woke and began to choke. He couldn't see me, of course.

Terrified, grabbing at his lips and his neck, he fell off the settle and tumbled, kicking, onto the floor amongst his own coins. I kept shoving. The ring inched further and further into his gullet. Then I got a twig out of his basket of kindling beside the empty hearth and poked the ring even further down. He'd never cough it up now. He couldn't even scream, just gurgle and gargle and thump his fists and heels on the floorboards. His face swelled and turned purple. His hands flopped limp. The choking noises faded to a faint wheeze.

I scooped up his money and left him, walked back around the corner and into my husband's quiet domain. Avoiding the solar, I rushed upstairs and piled the money under his flat pillow. I wondered if he'd guess where it came from. He heard something. He came to the solar door, wondering, and peered up the stairs.

But he couldn't see me. I'd been dead for nearly a month and it was more than three weeks since he'd been to my funeral. His brother had come to the funeral too. I'd watched them both from the vaulted ceiling above the altar, but not realising at the time that it was Godwin who had killed me. After slicing off my finger he had slit my throat with the same knife, watched my agony for a few moments, then left me to bleed over my clean washing.

He had no throat himself now, it was stuffed full of diamond, pearls and gold. A shame really, that no one else would ever have the pleasure of wearing such a beautiful ring, but then, after all, my father had stolen it from someone else in the first place. I'm not sure who. But it didn't matter anymore. The ring had moved on and now I was ready to do the same.

HAPPY EVER AFTER

by Helen Hollick

"SWAP you that pork pie for this chicken drumstick," the well-dressed older lady said to the young woman sitting next to her on one of the provided benches, and waving a napkin-wrapped offering which she had extracted from the small wicker hamper at her feet. "My cook is a dear lady, but she does tend to think that food like a common pork pie is somewhat beneath my status." She smiled, almost a grin, but that would have been a little *too* unlady-like for her to manage. She touched her large hat, a wild concoction of feathers and silk flowers, "I was born and raised in Leicestershire, not far from Mr Adcock's bakery and his famous pies. Mind, since marrying my dear Sir George and coming to live here in London, those childhood days have had to be put behind me." She almost managed a second grin, said in a pronounced country dialect, "Along with m' Leicestershire accent."

The young woman smiled and pushed back the tendrils of her black hair escaping her more modestly decorated straw bonnet as she nodded in agreement to the suggested swap. Did not let on that she had not tasted chicken for many a month. Even this pork pie and her meagre picnic fare was an exceptionally rare treat. Unlike the well-to-do ladies and gentlemen waiting patiently in this roped-off special seating area – accessed by ticket-holders only – she was dressed plainly, but immaculate and practical for a potential long wait until the procession passed by.

"They have a good day for it, at least," the older woman said, munching the pie and scattering pastry crumbs all over her skirt. She nodded towards the bunting and flags fluttering in the stiff breeze that also herded a few puffed, white clouds across the sapphire blue sky. "A bit blowy, perhaps, but no sign of rain."

"It poured at his first wedding," another woman sitting behind them said. "I got soaked to the bone, but it was worth it. The processions, then, were wonderful, and she – well the bride was the prettiest little thing I had ever set eyes on. I swear that her hair was spun gold. They say this second wedding is to be less extravagant, the essentials only."

The young woman suppressed a scornful snort. Less extravagant? Was that likely? Not with the Prince's penchant for opulent public display!

"Well we have to show our appreciation for his new bride, do we not?" the older woman's companion said, leaning forward and scattering raisins from her slab of fruit-cake everywhere. The wild birds would be having a feast once everyone had gone home. "After all, she will be our next queen when the king passes, God bless him."

The first woman discretely crossed herself. "He is getting quite frail, they say, poor man; but the Prince will make a fine king when his time comes. Such a shame what happened, though." She pursed her lips then tutted a couple of times, while wiping her fingers on a linen napkin. "His first wife was more suited to the role than this new little maid. She seems to be such a quiet mouse. Though dutiful, I hear tell."

"Aye," said another woman, joining in the conversation, "It is a great sadness that the first dear girl passed away so young."

"Such a wicked accident – to break her neck falling down the stairs like that," said the first woman.

"Tripped, they say."

"I heard," the young woman interrupted, discretely wiping her own greasy fingers on an old, but clean, cotton square, "that he pushed her."

The elder women looked at her, wide-eyed, open-mouthed. Quite askance. Then they all spoke at once.

"No!"

"He would not do such a thing!"

"You are treading near treason my girl!"

"He is the most charming, pleasant young man!"

"Kind, courteous, thoughtful ..."

"He would *never* do such a thing!"

The young woman let the outrage subside. "All that is his *public* face, the stories you read in the news-sheets. He is entirely different behind closed palace doors. He pushed her, and got away with it because he is the heir to the throne." Did not add, *And a manipulative little bastard.*

Several tuts of disapproval.

"And just how," challenged one of the women, "would *you* be knowing all this? Know someone inside the palace, do you?" It was meant as crushing sarcasm.

The young girl smiled, bit into a crunchy green apple, chewed, swallowed. "As it happens, yes, I do. I used to be there."

There were a couple of gasps and an eager moving forward to hear better. The tickets for this special area had cost several shillings and a chance of any bonus gossip for additional value for money was pounced upon, even if it came from someone who was obviously of the servile class.

"He might be a prince," the young woman went on, in between mouthfuls of apple, "but he is also an arrogant prig. He wants – no demands – his own way in everything." She paused, looked meaningfully at the women, one by one, "And I mean *everything*. Oh, he appears to be charming, romantic and caring whenever he is in public, but in private he is cruel and unkind. For his poor bride, once he owned her, he controlled everything she did. He demanded that his every wish was to be instantly obeyed, and if it is was not, he lashed out with his tongue, hand, fist or boot. Most of the servants, the female ones anyway, are terrified of him." She lowered her voice, "The male staff ensure, as much as possible, that the younger females are always chaperoned when in his presence. Even down to the lowest scullery maids going about their duties. Though, fortunately, the prince is rarely from his bed before noon, so the servants get as much done before then as they can."

More gasps of astonishment.

The young woman tucked the apple core neatly into the piece of cloth and put both into her holdall, buckled the clasp and nodded. "He ordered his wife what to eat or not to eat; what to wear, what to do. Who she could or could not see. He would not permit her to retain contact with any of her friends or family. He had the last say in *everything*. Oh, he was charming before the wedding, but his gentlemanly behaviour when in public is all a play-act. Once the wedding band was on her finger he had got what he wanted ... to own her ... and proceeded to make her life an utter misery."

The pork pie woman shook her head. "I do not believe it."

"He even beat her if she did not comply."

"No!"

"Never!"

The young woman nodded again firmly. "I saw the bruises. The welts across her back. He used his riding crop on her more than once."

Another woman joined in, her voice deliberately low as she whispered, "I think it is true. Do you not remember a bruise on her cheek that time they went to the opera? A few weeks before she died? It was mentioned in all the news-sheets. The palace said she had 'suffered an unfortunate accident with a cupboard door'."

The young woman snorted, said, "Soon after, she 'fell' down the stairs and broke her neck."

The elder women tutted or pursed their lips and nodded sagely. One said: "The funeral was such a sad occasion. I was here in this same spot, watched the cortège pass by. We all wept when the prince walked so solemnly behind the casket. His tears streamed down his face. I remember it well."

"Crocodile tears," said the young woman. "He did not mourn for long after the funeral did he?"

"That is true," someone agreed.

"What else can you tell us?" Pork Pie woman asked, eagerly.

The young woman shrugged. "I do not know anything else. I left the palace soon after the 'accident'."

Any further curiosity or questions were cut short by the sound of approaching hooves and blaring trumpets. There was a general rustling and getting to feet throughout the crowds thronging each side of the main thoroughfare leading to the cathedral. Picnic hampers were hastily shoved aside, to be replaced by little flags on wooden sticks, the waiting spectators eagerly surging forward, cheers hurling into the air along with tossed flowers and a variety of shouted good wishes.

The glass wedding coach rumbled past, flanked by smart soldiers dressed in their best uniforms.

The woman inside, a petite, demure lass who looked more like a girl than a woman grown, waved and smiled shyly at the well-wishers lining the route.

She was gone, a sigh of satisfaction swept through the crowd.

"Did you see her?"

"So pretty!"

"Looked like a lot of lace on that bodice."

"The diamonds in that tiara!"

"Aye, and did you catch a glimpse of the necklace?"

"I wonder how long her veil and train will be."

"What is the dress like? It looked like silk."

"I cannot wait to read about it in the news-sheets tomorrow."

The young woman listened to the excited chatter and exchange of opinions, but did not join in. Instead, she clutched her home-made patchwork rag-bag to her chest and kept her thoughts to herself. The young bride was indeed shy and demure, and more important, well trained in compliance and duty. She was not the type to naysay the prince, would be breeding as soon as may be and devote herself to the dozen or so children that she would have. A little mouse, the complete opposite to that first, unfortunate, wife who had held her own mind and who had refused to bow to the whims of a bully. Even if he were a royal prince.

The couple, once married and joined one to the other, would be returning to the palace via a different route. Many in the crowds began to push and squirm their way to a new vantage point, but the young woman had seen all she had wanted to see. She walked with a light step across the grass of the park, and headed for the less wealthy part of the city.

It was a long walk. Her rented home was one of a terraced row of old houses. Two up, two down, the only thing different for each, the extent of the worn, flaking paint on the doors and grimed window panes. The narrow street was shabby, not a slum, but not affluent either. Grubby curtains twitched as, head erect, she walked by. She and her husband were regarded as outsiders. Each morning he went off to work in a modest button maker's shop near St James; she busied herself with dressmaking and kept her house spotlessly clean. She took the door key from where it nestled securely inside her coat pocket and let herself into the house.

The front door led straight into the living room. Beyond, a tiny but neat kitchen. Upstairs one larger bedroom and another the size of a cupboard. She smiled, there was a posy of fresh flowers in what served as a glass vase on the dining table. A white linen cloth, exquisitely embroidered with little blue and red flowers hid the scratches that were gouged into the old wood. She could hear her husband out in the kitchen putting the kettle on to boil on the wood-burner stove. He appeared through the curtain that served as a door, wiping his wet hands with a towel.

"I've put the mutton stew to cook," he said as he walked across the faded, worn carpet to kiss her on the cheek and take her bonnet and coat, which he hung on a peg beside the front door. "Was it good to watch?"

She sat in one of the two shabby armchairs and removed her shoes. Her feet were aching from the walk. "I talked to some nice ladies, we swapped picnics."

"Did you see his new bride?"

"Oh yes. From what I know of her she will not gainsay him. Good luck to her, I say. She'll breed him lots of children and relish being a doting mama with no mind of her own beyond her brood of spoilt sons and daughters."

Her partner – he was not her husband, although not one of the neighbours knew this – sat on the arm of the chair and took her hand in his, kissed the gold-plaited band on her finger that sat there for propriety's sake. "You do not envy her then?" he asked.

The young woman looked up at him, her blue eyes wide with laughter. She tossed back a wisp of her dyed hair, some of the original blonde was showing through at the roots.

"What? Not in the slightest. I pity her. I had a lucky escape, got out before it was too late. I was not going to risk another sprained ankle because of being pushed down those stairs a second time. He took my threat that I would expose him to the news-sheets most seriously."

She nodded towards one of the drawers in the sideboard, a large ugly old thing that, like the table and armchairs, had come with the house. "I think," she said slowly, "we have kept our heads down long enough. It is time we moved on. The tale of my death is accepted, no one knows of the secret annulment or that the funeral was nothing but an arranged sham. All evidence of the truth has been destroyed; *he* has seen to that." She snorted contempt, "He strutted around wearing his widower's weeds with false solemnity and doesn't want me to reappear into his life any more than I want to. We've enough squirrelled away in that drawer from the money he paid me to disappear and keep quiet. It's time we started a new life somewhere far, far away from here. The Colonies perhaps?"

She smiled at the man beside her, rose from the chair and removed the posy of flowers from their unusual holder. She picked it up, her smile a combination of amusement, satisfaction and malice, then hurled it towards the tiny brick fireplace where the glass vessel shattered into a myriad of pieces. She picked up its twin and hurled that too, enjoying the sound of shattering destruction.

"I promised myself," she said to the man she had always loved (but had not realised it until it was too late) "that on the day I was truly set free of my mistake of a marriage, I would smash those bloody awful, bloody uncomfortable, fancy glass slippers that the control-freak bastard prince made me wear."

Buttons, as he was nicknamed because of his employment as a master button-maker, smiled, kissed her. "I love you Cindy. Love you lots and lots."

And that is how the *real* story of Prince Charming and Cinderella ends. Happy Ever After – but not *quite* as the fairy tale claims!

ACKNOWLEDGMENTS

How often do you see the words "This book would not have been possible without ..." ? Never have those words been truer.

To Helen Hollick, Barbara Gaskell Denvil and her daughter Gill Trewick. I cannot thank you enough for thinking about me, discussing me (behind my back!), offering the chance of publication and for the love, advice and support that you all gave me throughout the process. If you like Historical Fiction I can heartily recommend both Helen's and Barbara's books.

To my children Dan, Samantha, Donna and Aimee for their ever-present support.

To my dear friend Carolyn Ann Hipkiss who always read my stories with an open mind

As well as the two authors mentioned above, I must give mention to some selected Indie authors who have read my works and always offered encouragement and advice and always in the kindest way. These lovely people are in themselves really great writers and I present them in no particular order:

Annie Whitehead, Alison Morton, Anna Belfrage, Mercedes Rochelle, Kara Pohlkamp, Kimberley Jordan Reeman, Susan Grossey, Deborah Swift, Jane Harlond

ABOUT THE AUTHORS

RICHARD TEARLE

Richard was born in Muswell Hill, north London and the king deigned to put his stamp on his birth certificate. He grew up in the age of steam trains, trolley buses. And Tottenham Hotspur rewarded his support by winning The Double.

Richard's father was a clerk with the Electricity Board and his mother took in typing. She was also an accomplished pianist and gave Richard a love of music that has stayed with him throughout his life.

Richard left school and joined the Ever Ready Co (GB Ltd) before moving on to the Performing Right Society. He had a couple of spells in the dole queue before finishing his working life with what was then the Benefits Agency. Now divorced, Richard has four wonderful children. He has lived in Highgate, Friern Barnet, Barnet, Margate, Ramsgate and now, Lichfield. Following retirement he has spent a lot of time visiting historical places that have always fascinated him. As well as reviewing for Discovering Diamonds – the best job he ever had.

Richard's only published work until now, has been a short story that was included in an anthology of stories about Richard III entitled 'Right Trusty and Well Beloved.' It is reproduced here.

Richard hopes to continue writing for many years to come.
DDRevs website: https://discoveringdiamonds.blogspot.com/
Slipstream Blog: https://rtslipstream.blogspot.com

HELEN HOLLICK

Helen Hollick lives on a thirteen-acre farm in Devon, England. Born in London, Helen wrote pony stories as a teenager, moved to science-fiction and fantasy, and while working in the local library discovered historical fiction. She was first accepted for publication by William Heineman in 1993 with her *Pendragon's Banner* Arthurian Trilogy, and then her two 1066-era historical novels, the second of which about Queen Emma, *The Forever Queen* (UK title *A Hollow Crown*) became a *USA Today* bestseller. She also writes the *Sea Witch Voyages*; pirate-based nautical adventures with a touch of fantasy, and has two non-fiction books published about pirates and smugglers.

Helen enjoys helping indie/self-published authors receive the attention they deserve, and to this end founded the historical novel review blog *Discovering Diamonds* in 2017. To help her, she has a superb team of dedicated assistants and eager reviewers, one of whom is Richard Tearle, the Senior Reviewer. Whether for his experience, status, or his age has not yet been confirmed...

Website: www.helenhollick.net

Newsletter Subscription: http://tinyletter.com/HelenHollick

Main Blog: www.ofhistoryandkings.blogspot.com

Amazon Author Page (Universal Link) http://viewauthor.at/HelenHollick

Twitter: @HelenHollick

Discovering Diamonds Historical Fiction Review Blog (submissions welcome) : https://discoveringdiamonds.blogspot.co.uk/

Barbara Gaskell Denvil is a multi-award-winning author of historical fiction, mystery, suspense and fantasy. Now, for the first time, she is also writing children's fantasy, combining the genres she loves, historical and adventure with fantasy.

Having been born into a literary family where bookshelves filled every room, she grew up assuming that writing would be her career. Barbara began writing when she was extremely young and then went to work in the British Museum Library, with ancient folios and manuscripts. This cemented her love of both literature and history. Moving on to work in traditional publishing, scripting, reviewing, editing and publishing many articles and short stories.

Her books now alternate between fantasy and historical fiction, drama, mystery, adventure and romance, with a passion for medieval settings and historical accuracy.

Miss Gaskell Denvil's work has been traditionally published by Simon & Schuster, but she now favours self-publishing as it gives the huge satisfaction of individual control. And personal choice of genre and artistic inspiration.

You can find out more about Barbara and her books at https://barbaragaskelldenvil.com or find her on Amazon here.

Printed in Poland
by Amazon Fulfillment
Poland Sp. z o.o., Wrocław

57519120R00070